MW00943627

Blind to Blood

Rachel,

Please read, and let
me know what you
think!

[signature]

by

George Kramer

GEORGE KRAMER

Disclaimer

Age restrictions for removal of grafts are ever changing; they are in a constant flux. What can be removed from a donor can change dependent upon what graft is needed at the time. My point is the story is fiction, but based on medical facts. However, some of the medical facts are subject to alteration. My intent was to create a story based on what I did at one time. Whether or not it's applicable today is not what my intention was, or is, today. I have taken certain liberties with the story line, so I am not responsible for any intentional or unintentional errors, or consequences.

While Ben Berstgel was brutal, I want to strongly emphasize the recovery of tissue is done in a controlled environment, and everything possible is done to ensure the safe handling and removal of people's loved ones donation.

Other books by George Kramer

ebooks only:

My little girl and her Musings

More of Caris's Musings

Poetry:

What is the written word for?

Pondering Existence

ebooks and print books:

YA Fantasy:

Arcadis: Prophecy (Book One)

Arcadis: War (Book Two)

Arcadis: Decimation (Book Three)

Arcadis: Emperor of all, Emperor of none (Book Four)

Arcadis: Convergence (Book Five)

Arcadis: To Walk Among the Gods (Book six)

All books can be found at:

www.amazon.com/author/georgekramer

If you would like to chat with the author, please send email to:

georgekramerauthor@gmail.com

Great read! It flows, draws you in, and creeps you out the whole way! I get told all the time I'm emotionless from the military and things I've done. But this book made my skin crawl and really gave me the sensation of visual stimulation!

Mark Isbell, Veteran owned business in Noblesville, IN. www.hoosierpoleandflag.com

Dedication

A great deal of people went into making this book. First, and foremost, are my wife and daughter. They provided me with ample time to write with little distraction. When I am in the writing mode, on occasion, they will ask me to stop writing, and hang out with them.

Greg Hebert has been wonderful in providing all of the author pictures on the back cover (including this one), besides the first Arcadis book. Additionally, Greg Hebert Photography helped me with the book cover, which was no easy task. His attention to detail and his serious commitment to my project made the experience much more pleasurable. I would highly recommend Greg. His friend, Jason McGee, was instrumental as well. His expertise, coupled with his equipment, helped ensure a smooth experience. Thanks go to Ben Bastnagel and Brittany Schott for modeling. Great work!

As usual I have certain people I really like to brainstorm with. Ray Wininger, Zach Penrod Ben Bastnagel, Corey Shotwell, and Greg Hebert make up the gist of my group. Thank you, guys!

A big thank you goes to Danielle Love for making sure my medical facts concerning tissue removal were accurate and up to date. I had the pleasure of working with Danny, and she is one of the best tissue procurement specialists I have ever had the pleasure of working alongside.

I want to thank my friends who wanted to be in my book, either as someone that was killed, mentioned, or a red herring. Jen Walker, Ben Bastnagel, Andre King, Jenni Nazimek, AJ Mandary, Brittany Schott, Ray Wininger, and an honorable mention goes to Donna Perry Graybosch.

I would like to thank my editor Angela Rackard Campbell for editing my book. I appreciated her commitment to see this book edited and published!

Table of Contents

January 3rd

My name is Ben Berstgel, and this is my story of how I was able to surgically remove body parts, and how I was able to find the people to do it to. Do you know what the best part was? I liked it. I really liked to do it while they were awake too. That last fact happened unintentionally, as you will read later. Call me mad, call me insane. It doesn't matter because I can't do it anymore. As a matter of fact, I can barely pick up a knife to cut anything, or change clothes. Detective Jay Club had seen to that! But I digress. I will tend to deviate from time to time in this journal as I go on tangents. Not to fear! You will get your exclusive, dear readers.

A question may come to your mind. How can I relate this bit of history to you when I barely have use of my hands? An astute mind! I am using the popular software that takes my words and puts them in sentences. Another question may cross the threshold of your consciousness. How did I learn how to surgically remove various upper and lower bones, tendons, veins, Peritoneal membrane (which is the lining that holds your intestines in place), Pericardium (a thin membrane which envelopes the heart), Skin, Heart, and Mandible (Jawbone)? That's an excellent question, readers! Before I answer your important query, I must first rid myself of the orderly that likes to come by to make sure I am *following procedures*, and behaving. Really? Didn't he know when I legitimately removed body parts; it was a tightly regulated industry that had strict procedures and protocols? The S.O.P.'s (Standard Operating Procedures) were constantly updated, and we had to read them, and sign off that we had read them? No, of course he didn't know that. So, I know how to follow procedures, thank you very much. Mr. Orderly was a big man. He was tall, and had a belly that protruded well past what I thought was humanely possible. He always wore the same white shirt, white pants, with his white shoes. His hair was even white, and combed to the side. He was an ass who would come by my room to taunt me. If I were napping during the day, he would come by with his baton, smash my door with it, wake me up, and then apologize without conviction. He once smashed my leg with his baton, and broke it because he was in a bad mood. It took months to heal correctly! He told everyone I had fallen. If only I had my medical bag with me, and the use of my hands... Where was I? Oh yes, how did I become what is termed as either a recovery tech or what I liked better, a tissue procurement specialist? The latter sounded more sophisticated. I was with my mother, whom I abhor, at the hospital after one of her usual drunken stupors. She inevitably hurt herself. It was there I saw three people in surgical scrubs. They were carrying a shitload of medical things like bio-hazard boxes, covered tubs and an assortment of stuff I had no clue what they were, but were obviously heavy because they brought in a four-wheeled cart to move everything. The person in charge went to talk to the nurse at the ER desk while the other two were just standing idly by. I decided to talk to them. However, once I moved several feet away from my mother, she yelled for me to stay. I ignored her even though her voice continued to escalate in a grating, irritating manner. I swear if I had owned a gun, I would have pulled the trigger on her right there and then, and blew her fucking brains out. I could devote several journals with just her antics. Anyway, I calmly went to the man and woman, and started chatting. They seemed unwilling to talk to me. They tried to avoid eye contact with me. Why do you think that is, dear readers? Could it be from the huge dark brown and yellow discoloration that encompassed the whole left side of my body? They clearly saw my face, throat, and my arms that the T-shirt didn't cover. I'll allocate an entry for that subject later! What I managed to glean from the reluctant shits was they recovered tissue from the dead bodies in hospitals, morgues, funeral homes, and coroner's offices for donation. They were paged out when they were on call, and had an hour to get to the office. Then they were told where they were going, and what body parts were going to be removed. At that point, the person in charge came back. He did a half nod to me, and told the others to follow him. How I wanted to follow them rather than listen to my mother's continuous ranting! I returned to my seat, ignoring my mother's outbursts. All I could think about was cutting out people's body parts, and actually getting paid to do it. I grinned with devilish delight.

I told you from the start, readers, how I surgically removed body parts. There had to be a starting point. From there, the rest had been easy. I lied. I went to the internet, found the closest procurement business, and gave them a call. I told them I had a medical background, and was interested in a position. I was granted an interview. I sat down with the director and told him I was in school to become a certified surgical technologist. Obviously, I had to do research in case they asked questions. Prior to reading about it online, I had never heard of a C.S.T. (In a nutshell, they are the people that hand the surgeons the surgical instruments). I filled out an application, paid someone on the internet to alter records at the nearest vocational school to make it look legit, and told the director I would give him references upon request. He hired me but I had to wait three agonizing weeks before I was allowed to start.

The director, a sap named Tony Roth, was tall and thin. His hair was severely receded which gave him an appearance of being older. He brought me over and introduced me to the others that worked there. I will not bore you to death with their trivial lives or detail their accomplishments. Why? Because I'm here to relate to you how, and why, I killed people for fun and for profit!

Most of the staff was nice enough, and shook hands with me but they concentrated on my left side with the humongous dark brown and yellow birthmark. I felt like yelling at them it wasn't my fault. I was born with it and my father left my mother because of it, which caused her to drink excessively and blame me. But I didn't. I remained placid because I wanted to learn how to cut out people's body parts. One person, Michael Banner, refused to shake hands with me. He didn't even look at me. At this point readers, wouldn't you understand the embarrassment and hatred that emanated from me?

The first thing I had to do was read thousands of pages of S.O.P.'s before I was allowed to go out and harvest. It took a week. It was the longest week of my life. During that week of misery, I tried to make friends with some of these people. Not an easy task. One of them in particular made no bones (no pun intended readers!) about how he felt about me. When the others did open up, all they talked about was about tissue. Admittedly, I had learned a great deal. I learned despite the heart and skin being Organs, when a person died, they were considered tissue. I learned a plethora of the background on what it takes for the facilitator to do to even get a team to go on a recovery.

Did you know, dear readers, that when someone died at a hospital, it's the law the nurse must call the organ, eye and tissue banks and speak to the respective person from each group? Obviously, the representative from the Organ Company spoke first, and then the eye bank's representative would have a three-way conversation with our facilitator (tissue), and the nurse who had called. The facilitators are also responsible for doing pre-audits on medical charts. I may bore you with these medical details but the more I inform you, the better you'll understand my need for stealth when I removed body parts, called grafts, from humans. The FDA highly regulates the organ, eye, and tissue industries. Hence my covertness in finding humans, targeting certain ones (e.g. taller people, more often than not, provide more skin removal and longer saphenous veins).

Another question may come to your shrewd mind. Where did I send the grafts once I surgically removed them? Truth be told, I don't know. I used to purloin corrugated cardboard boxes from the tissue place, add several thick clear bags, put ice in them (stole the ice too!) and put the bones, tendons, hearts, and all the other body parts into the bags. I sealed them up, and left them in a designated spot that was provided by my clandestine customer. My secret client was from an anonymous email at work. They promised me additional money if I would steal some of the grafts when I came back from a recovery, and sent it to a predetermined location. Obviously, I couldn't do that because I would have been caught right away. Everything had to be accounted for. Every graft that was removed was recorded, and put in the donor's chart. I told my future client I couldn't do that, but I was more than willing to go out on my own, and provide them with grafts from ordinary people. At first, they were reluctant because once a person died; the facilitator had to call their family as soon as possible because there was a time limit on body parts and an age limit on certain grafts. The questionnaire the facilitator asked a next of kin, or a POA (power of attorney) concerned the deceased family history. If the person had cancer within the last five years, what type of cancer, any STD's, were they in a certain country between certain years, and a myriad of other questions. Based on the questions, the potential donor may be ruled out or may be a go. I understood all that, people. But as I told the client, *who the hell cares?* If someone needs their life enhanced, why not take a risk? Hell, I told them, sell them to countries which have less restrictive laws than we do. I received a reply a week later. My foray in taking people's lives was born.

Mind you, I had been doing tissue procurement for three years before that life changing email came across my desk. Whoever wrote to me was very convincing. It seemed as if they knew me. The main theme was I would get to kill people by surgically remove body parts, get paid, and live happily ever after. How they got my name, or knew of me, was none of my concern. The fact they wanted more grafts outside of the highly-regulated industry told me they were looking to augment their finances. And so was I. I have been paying my mother's rent, food, and her medical expenses, plus mine. Either I had to get rid of her (a viable option) or supplement my income. At that time, the latter was my choice. It was a difficult choice. My mother wore me out. I would have liked to take her permanently out.

Sorry reader, I tire easily because it's hard to exercise without the use of my hands. I grow weary relating my tale to you. I will commence on another date.

January 5th

It is one thirty in the morning and I can't sleep. Mr. Orderly came by but I pretended to be asleep. He banged my bed with his damned asp to try to rouse me. He shined a flashlight in my face but I didn't move a muscle. I have heard of his exploits with other patients. I hoped he didn't try anything on me. Finally, he left. I looked at my room and determined it was a right time to continue my journal. Some readers may wonder where I am incarcerated. I went on trial and was convicted but was ruled mentally ill. I was sentenced to this hellhole of what was once called a sanatorium but now called a hospital for the criminally insane. To me, it was semantics. I didn't mind the gray, chipped paint, or the water stained ceilings. The yellowed curtains allowed me to have some privacy. The ancient mattress hurt my ass, but I really didn't care as long as they fed me, and allowed me to write, or rather speak to my laptop. I think they allowed me to have a laptop because of my notoriety. The local press still camped outside the building in McCordsville, Indiana, hoping for a glimpse of the infamous person who skinned and de-boned people, and who was caught removing body parts off a girlfriend of a popular Detective. However, what I wanted to discuss in this particular entry was my skin discoloration and the taunting I received growing up. Like I stated previously, I was born with a dark brown and yellow skin discoloration on my entire left side of my body. My mother had told me the doctor had gasped when he saw the discoloration. My mother also told me she had cried. I'm sure it wasn't from joy of being a new mother, but rather the look on my father's face when he saw my abnormality. My mother told me my dad had told her I was an abomination, walked out of the room, and never came back. Whether any of that is true or not, I'll never know. All I knew was my father had left, and my mother was never the same, especially toward me. The neighborhood I lived in never embraced me either. Kids can be mean. I vividly recalled kids riding by my house throwing water balloons with diluted mustard in them. They smashed against my house, and spread the yellowish-brown liquid all over. To this day, there were still residual stains I couldn't get out. That was my nickname. Mustard. I was always in fights and often got beat up. You would think in high school things would calm down, kids would mature, and I would be left alone. Not the case. A kid named Claude Peterson was the equivalent in my social status. To rise above the bottom position meant to torture someone else to elevate their own status. He would push me into the lockers and call me names. If I tried to say something, I was punched in the mouth or the gut. On the last day of high school I had my locker open, and looked around to make sure no one was there. Guess what, readers? I wasn't alone.

I think it was Claude that pushed me from behind. He, or someone, pushed me *into* the locker and closed the door. I was too tall for the locker, which made it difficult to remain erect inside. I banged on the door for what seemed like hours. I was in there so long I pissed and defecated in my pants. Finally, after an indeterminate amount of time, a teacher happened to walk by and heard my banging. He rushed to the office to get a set of keys to unlock the door. When he let me out, I cried. The teacher, Mr. Astor, gagged from the smell that was emanating from me. He asked if I wanted him to call my parents to pick me up. I declined through sobs. I ran all the way home. When I entered my abode, my mom was passed out in her recliner with the television blaring, and liquor bottles littered all over the floor. It was then my hatred for humanity had cemented. Mind you, I didn't like people prior to being locked in a locker, but the feeling that I would never fit in solidified. I quickly ran up the stairs, showered, changed clothes, walked to my bed and sat down. Looking around, I knew I didn't have a lot of toys or stuffed animals because my mom spent all of her welfare money, on alcohol. My bedroom lacked curtains so I used midnight blue shower towels and hung them. My bed was stained of piss because I used to wet my bed because of the beatings I received when I was younger. My mom had a temper, and when she would drink in excess, she would come in my room, blame me for our problems, and promptly beat me with my own belt. That is, until I got old enough to threaten her. These days she ranted, and passed out in her chair.

During the summer, after high school was over, Claude got a car. He would drive around my house and moon me. His friends would throw beer bottles on my lawn. Before I had to clean all of bottles up, my mother would demand I take all of the remaining beer in all of the cans and combine them so she could drink it. One fateful day, I was walking to the store to buy my mother cigarettes and beer when Claude and his friends passed by. They slowed down and backed up when they saw me. Claude parked his car and jumped out, along with his buddies. To say I was frightened would have been an understatement. Two of the guys grabbed my arms and held them behind my back. Claude came to me, grinned, and took something out of his back pocket. It was a makeup kit. He told me it was his sister's and he thought I could use some to hide my birthmark. I squirmed as the brush came closer to my face. Another boy punched me in the stomach, and I almost puked. Claude put makeup on the left side of my face but left the rest of the birthmark alone. He remarked it looked better than my mustard face. I was pushed to the ground as they laughed and took off. I went back home to remove the makeup while my mother demanded to know where her cigarettes and beer were. I told her to shut up, and that I would get them later. God, I hated my mother, Claude, and the rest of my former classmates. How I wanted to get rid of their leader, Claude! I thought about Claude, and how he thought he was so cool with his car. Hmm, cars. An idea surfaced. I walked to the library to do some research. I wanted to learn about brakes on cars. If my research was successful, Claude's last days on earth were numbered. I read all I could on brake lines until it was time for the library to close. I didn't take any books out, of course, to cover my tracks, and the fact I had a photographic memory. When it was dark, I snuck to Claude's house, and went underneath his car. It took some time to find the brake line because I didn't want to shine any light, and took out a syringe I had stolen from my mother's diabetic kit. She had syringes of varying sizes and I picked the smallest needle that attached to the syringe. I doubted she would miss one. I found the upper part of the brake line where it was attached with a clamp. I filled the syringe with air, and stuck the thin tip of the needle just below the clamp, forced the needle into the hose, and pushed the air into the brake line. I repeated the process for nearly thirty minutes, stopping occasionally to give my arms and shoulders a rest. I slithered out from under the car and walked nonchalantly home pleased with myself. The next morning I awoke one happy person. For the first time, I felt I did something worthwhile. I purposely stayed home for the next couple of days to make sure I wasn't around when Claude's car brakes wouldn't respond.

I heard the crash the second day. I looked at the clock on the wall. Four thirteen in the afternoon. The accident happened several houses down from me. I put on my best poker face and walked to the scene. I listened in on the conversations. Claude had been going over the speed limit and tried to slow down at the stop sign. He was unable to stop and a van had careened into his side of the vehicle. The firemen had to use a special tool to remove the driver's side of the door, and remove his lifeless body. I acted shocked and put my hand to my mouth but in actuality, I was very happy. I had surmised the police would find out about the history between Claude and myself, and come knocking. It hadn't taken long. Three days later, there was a knock on my door. I presumed my mother would be passed out and I would answer the door. To my surprise, my mother was up and she was leaning against the door frame. Her flowered nightgown was sleeveless, and the flesh on her arms hung low even though she was thin. Her bony kneecaps protruded from her ugly nightie. Her hair was long and stringy. When a strong breeze went by her, her hair stuck in place. I hurried to the door, not wanting the police to see my living conditions. They asked if they could come in. My mother told them no, but I was more than willing to go down to the police station and speak to them. Thankfully, the questions were short and to the point. They asked where I was when Claude's car crashed. I had an alibi, at home with my mother. They asked about the altercations Claude and I had. I pointed out it was kids' stuff, and he didn't mean anything by it. Bullying was bullying. The police seemed to believe me. I was allowed to leave. It was shortly thereafter I realized I got away with my first murder.

January 9th

After rereading the last entry, I realized I still enjoyed the memory of killing Claude. Now, as an adult, I surmised the proclivity for violence had always been with me. With Claude, it brought it to the surface. The sense of excitement that I could inflict pain on someone versus the other way around stimulated me into seeking over venues. Since I didn't work at the time I went to the library and read up on serial killers. There were a few commonalities between them. The only one I didn't do, or think to do, was kill animals, bugs, or insects. But the common theme with them, and me, was the urge to hurt, maim, or kill people. Soon the urge to kill grew stronger. However, I didn't have a clue as to how, or who. Until, of course, I watched my first tissue procurement. After reading the boring S.O.P.'s I got to go on my first recovery. I learned I was to observe the first three cases, and then it was time for me to start cutting. It was sink or swim.

I received my first phone call for a tissue recovery because I didn't have a set time to go to the office. I was on call and had to pick my days, and if I wanted twelve or twenty-four hour shifts. As a result, I had an hour to get to the tissue place. By the time we changed into surgical scrubs, packed for the case, drove to the hospital, talked to the nurse, and went to the morgue, my first procurement was at two forty in the morning. I went to the morgue, without any knowledge of how I was going to react. The police officer opened the morgue door, wrote down our names, and the time we entered. I looked around because I had never been in a morgue before. I wondered, as I surveyed my surroundings, if Claude had been in a similar room. That brought a smile to my lips.

It was a very small room. On television shows, morgues appeared huge. At this particular hospital, it was tiny. There was a cooling vent leading to the door that housed the body or bodies. One of the people I was with told me the freezer only held two bodies at a time, but some morgues can hold thirty or more. To the right of the freezer was a table with a sink attached to the head. I presumed the sink attachment was for autopsies. To the left were shelves that housed chemicals, and containers that had different body parts immersed with formaldehyde. That was all that was in the room. We barely had room to put our supplies. The officer left as one of my colleagues opened the freezer door. We saw a white zipped up body bag, and the dead person was in it. We pulled the drawer out until it wouldn't go out any further. Then one of the techs, the circulator, and me lifted the portly person onto the table with the sink. I had the honors of opening up the zip lock bag. I knew they wanted me to open the bag to gauge how I would react. They seemed disappointed I didn't hurl or run from the room. One of the people, from day one, always called me Mustard, seemed the most upset. I hated that fucker. I wished Michael Banner was the person on the table. Anyway, since the shelves that housed jars that had the body parts in them were out in the open, we had to use drapes, and duct tape them across the shelves so there wouldn't be any cross contamination. Obviously, we had to thoroughly wash our hands using aseptic techniques. Then we had to don our PPE (personal protection equipment), ask the circulator to start to aseptically give us our supplies, and we put them on the small tables after we had put sterile back table covers over them. Then the excitement commenced!

Uh oh, I hear that orderly banging his baton on a nearby room. I have to go. I will pretend to be asleep again. Mr. Orderly had to go! His intrusions upon my quiet time were annoying.

January 13th

The last few days were occupied with going to rehab for my hands. Slowly, ever so slowly, I was getting a little feeling and dexterity in them. The pain I was experiencing was probably pale compared to the people I procured grafts from. That was a good lead in to what I wanted to discuss with you. Like I mentioned in a previous entry, I was at the tissue company for three years when I was contacted via email. With my suggestion of finding a suitable third world country which had less restrictive regulations than America, and getting approval to start, I went about finding a suitable donor. How does one do this? Good question, readers. I feel like the teacher and you, the student! It took patience and keen observation. However, my first tissue kill would be a practice run, and I knew who I wanted to kill. No, it wasn't my mother, albeit I was inclined to think along those lines. Who, I thought to myself, was responsible for my miserable existence? My father. He was the one that ran out on me and my mother. We never heard from him again, but did we, readers? I knew where he lived. He sent my mother a Christmas card when I was ten, but my mother tore it up and threw it out. I snatched it from the garbage pail, and taped it back together. It seemed dear old dad was reminiscing, and wanted to get back together if she got rid of me. The envelope contained his address. What was interesting was he had a different last name than mine. Perhaps my mother, in her decaying mind, changed our last name back to Berstgel? Didn't know, did not care. It's not like I had a good rapport with my mother to ask such questions. My father's address was fifteen, twenty years ago, but I was betting he still lived there.

His name was Arthur Cooper, and I had scoped out his place for a week. I knew his routine by heart. His schedule never deviated. I arrived at his neighborhood around one thirty in the morning. I noticed the moon was obscured from the clouds, making it much darker. I drove slowly, not too slowly where a nosy neighbor could get a glimpse of my car, and of me. I found a parking spot a street over where it was more dark and desolate. Tree limbs hung over which somewhat concealed my car. I grabbed my medical bag and supplies, and slipped out the car door. I walked nonchalantly as fear and elation gripped me at the same time. I hadn't felt this way since I purposely tinkered with Claude's brakes over a decade ago. After a few agonizing minutes, I came upon his abode and went to the back alley to Arthur's quiet, dark home. I had watched Arthur through the back windows of the house from the alleyway for several days before making my move tonight, long enough to see through the high-tech night binoculars from the alleyway when Cooper had set the house alarm code before going to bed. I had checked it several other nights to make certain I knew the code and wouldn't trip the alarm by mistake when I snuck in.

The only sound I could discern was from people's automated sprinkler system. From the back door, I could see his kitchen. There was a small table in there with a light with a soft glow light bulb. Arthur was sitting down with his back to me. He got up, went to the fridge and was looking through it. The fact the intended target was awake, and would be aware, thrilled me to no end. I deemed it was now or never. My heart was racing as I opened my medical bag, quickly put on a pair of gloves, a black ski mask, and opened up a clear plastic bag that had rag doused with a homemade concoction of ether (ethyl alcohol and sulfuric acid). I took a deep breath, plugged the alarm code numbers slowly, ever so slowly to ensure I didn't push any by mistake, and then carefully and quietly, I continued into the doorway near the kitchen. I could just make out the wretched Arthur Cooper in there, standing at the kitchen counter, with his back to me. It looked like he was making a sandwich. It hadn't been how I had planned it, but that was fine with me. In fact, it only made this first attempt more exciting, absolutely exhilarating. I checked to make sure I still had my bag in hand, that it hadn't spilled open. Silly thought, but I wasn't taking any chances I might get this wrong. It all had to be just perfect.

I bolted into the kitchen, came up behind him

and shoved the ether-soaked rag under his nose, holding his neck in a choke-hold while Arthur struggled. It wasn't long before the soaked rag took all of the fight out of him, and his body went limp. I let him fall to the floor. He smelled as though he hadn't taken a shower in weeks. I grabbed his hands and dragged the body out of the kitchen into the darkened living room. The curtains were mostly closed. There was a sliver of light that shone in his living room which provided an adequate amount of illumination. I carefully and methodically removed Arthur's clothing and placed them in a large plastic bag. I looked at the pathetic body on the floor and kicked him in his testicles, just for the fun of it. The only thing that could have made the experience better would have been for Arthur to be awake for the abuse. But if he were awake, he would start screaming. I took out a second doused rag of ether, and put it under my father's nose, hoping to keep him sedated. Satisfied, I was now going to surgically remove Arthur's skin.

His age made his heart and other tissues ineligible, but the client only wanted skin at this point. I debated the merit of taking everything out of him just to get back at him for leaving me at birth, but opted not to. This was my first time without the aid of another tech, that meant I had to do everything myself, and I wanted to hurry up. First, I turned on his television to mask the impending noise. Certain the old man was sedated; it was time to work my magic. I took out back table covers, and laid two of them across the floor, one for Arthur, the other to place my supplies. I struggled to place Arthur's body on top of the first sterile back table cover. Once that was accomplished, I took out the dermatome, which would remove the skin; then I removed the liquid soap, or 4% CHG, disposable razor blades, and an assortment of other surgical instruments I would need. Slowly, with the precision of a skilled surgeon, I shaved my father's back (obviously the ether rag was still on his nose, but I had made sure he was still able to breathe). I continued down the old man's buttocks and finally ended at the Achilles tendon (the heel). Then I rolled him on his back, and shaved his calves, up his inner thigh, to his crotch. After he was shaven, and the hairs were to one side, I had to move him back on his stomach. Then I cleansed the old man's skin on his back and legs with the 4% CHG using small, circular motions. Back in the day they used to towel dry the skin with sterile towels, but the studies found if you keep the CHG on; it is more effective with bacteria control. See, dear readers? I am educating you while basking in my glory! Then I poured mineral oil on his posterior (back), and smoothed it over the surface of his skin. I made sure there was a lot of mineral oil. I liked how his skin shined, even in the dimly lit room. The part I love best came next: I picked up the dermatome, turned it on, and put the vibrating machine with the three inch super sharp razor against the top part of the man's shoulder. I angled it at a thirty-degree angle, and with precision, moved the dermatome downward and removed a long, thin strip of bloody and fresh skin from Arthur's back. I put the skin in a container that held a solution to keep the skin as sterile as possible. I looked at my handiwork and declared, "Absolutely glorious!" I continued removing the old man's skin with relish. I heard some grunts as his skin was been surgically detached, but he never awoke because the ether rag was on his nose all the time.

After I removed his skin from his posterior, I did the same to his anterior (front), avoiding the belly because his skin was too soft to get a decent amount. There were more than the three-square feet that was the minimum they wanted me to take, which pleased me. After I made damned sure all traces of my existence were removed, I decided to play a little game with the officers who were eventually going to find him. I put on another gown with two pairs of gloves, booties, and a hat. I dragged my father's bleeding body on his carpet to one of his chairs at his dining room table. With difficulty, I dragged Arthur up on to the chair, and leaned him back. I took my gloved fingers, and forced a smile on his face. I walked carefully back to his kitchen, found a plate, fork, and knife. I put those items on the table next to

24

him as if he were waiting for someone to make him dinner, albeit he was in the nude. I checked my handiwork, nodded my approval, then gathered up everything, and put them in a garbage bag I had brought. I checked for a pulse, but there was none. I guess his old body couldn't take the suffering I gave him. Good riddance! I left quickly and quietly. It had taken longer than I wanted, but it was still dark when I exited his home. I struggled to walk with all of the equipment, but managed to get to my car, entered my vehicle where I had taken out the light out when the door opened. I slipped into the night, delighted I had my second kill, although this one was done with such meticulousness that I smiled all the way to the drop off, and deposited the body parts in the box with ice. From there I drove home in such a good mood, I actually had a good night's sleep.

January 30th

I now knew my life had purpose, dear readers. While work became a little more bearable, the sense of pleasure of killing my father never dissipated. Now, every time I went anywhere, and people looked at me with disdain because of my mustard discoloration, all I had to do was think to myself how easily I could make them suffer such exquisite pain. Usually a cruel smile surfaced as I walked away from them.

So, dear readers, what next? Well, this is a journal, and I have more stories to relate to you. Yesterday Mr. Orderly told me I had a phone call. Patients aren't allowed to have their own cell phones. The phone was a landline, which hung on the wall that was located in the hallway. Before I walked out the door, Mr. Orderly put his foot out, and tripped me. I fell face first. I was glad the carpet helped with the impact, but it still hurt like hell. My hands were useless to try to break the fall. Blood had trickled from my nose to my mouth. Mr. Orderly laughed as he walked away. The gentleman on the phone call was from a tabloid. He wanted to do an article about me. He lived in Hollywood, wanted to do an exclusive one on one interview. As I struggled holding the phone to my ear with my barely usable hands, I told him to piss off. He laughed it off, and tried to get me to talk by asking me the most baseless questions I have ever heard. Where the hell that guy received his degree, if he even had one, was beyond me. "How do you feel living in an insane asylum?" "What kind of food do they give you?" "Do you see a shrink?" were some of the inane questions he posed. Why yes, I love living in an asylum where the food is great, and I see a shrink three times a week. What a fucking pathetic loser. The next day I looked online, (Where my access is severely limited, and they heavily monitor where I can go. No facetime, skype or any other site you could call someone. They can see where I browse.) The idiotic reporter wrote I loved my accommodations, have full use of my hands, I couldn't wait to get out to commit more atrocities, while having an affair with the lady shrink. Later that day, I was unceremoniously brought in front of the warden, and grilled for two hours. I don't know if he believed my side or not, but the orderly (which I found out was named Steve) brought me back to my room where he beat me with his baton until I was black and blue. He purposely hit my gnarled hands several times. All my efforts of physical therapy were for naught. I withered in pain on my bed in the fetal position for the entire rest of the day and night. I probably would have to start therapy from scratch. Bastard!

February 1st

Why not start with my next victim since my client wanted more grafts. First, I want to get something off my chest. Because of my shyness due to my huge mustard discoloration, I often wore an over-sized hoodie and sunglasses. In some instances, such as when I was at the ER with my mother, she made me remove them. Additionally, I had never been with a woman. I was a virgin. Who better than a hooker could propel me into manhood? And then to harvest her? Wow! I was feeling like a million dollars! I drove over thirty miles to a place that was known to have hookers, according to someone I had overheard at work. I drove slowly, and glanced nonchalantly through my tinted windows. I looked on both sides of the street until I saw a lone woman walking. The hooker looked alone, and frightened on the deserted street. Her eyes darted back and forth. I checked my surroundings carefully, making sure no cars or people were nearby. I knew call girls had pimps but couldn't see him anywhere. The darkened streets had lampposts but they had no bulbs in them to light up my surroundings. I rolled down my window as I approached her. Quickly I conducted my business with her, found out her price for a lay, and drove her to the sleazy hotel a few miles away. I made sure she gave the money to the guy at the front office to pay for the room. When we entered the room, she turned on the light and gasped when she saw I had removed my hoodie and sunglasses to reveal my enormous dark yellow and brown birthmark, but she was a professional, and hid her repulsion well. While she may think me repulsive, she was attractive. She had creamy olive skin, black shoulder length black hair, blue eyes, full lips, and breasts men would drool over. She wasn't small, but she wasn't corpulent. She was perfect. Why this perfect specimen walked the streets was anyone's guess.

She asked me in a seductive voice, "So honey, do you like it fast and furious, or slow and easy?" She turned around, went to the window, and shut the dark green curtains. She walked to the nearest nightstand and turned on the lamp. The lighting was not too bright, not too dark. Perfect. She was setting herself up for her own demise.

I didn't look at her much because I had never been with a woman before, and was very nervous. The only thing I knew was she had very good skin. I could look at people at a glance and determine if they had good quality skin in an instant. This one qualified. I really wanted to tell her my life story, expel my frustration, and to tell her the truth; I was going to kill her and remove her skin. At this point readers, you would think I would turn around, and run for my life. But an electric current zipped through me. I felt more confident than I had in my entire life! "Please sit down before we begin."

She smiled. I noticed she had even white teeth. I wondered if prostitutes had dental or medical insurance. "Oh, the formal, get to know you type. Okay mister, it's your dime."

"Do you see the dark mustard color that runs along the left side of me?"

She did her best to smile. "Yeah, it's no big deal, honey. You should see some of the freaks I fuck."

"Uh, thanks? My father called me an abomination. Do you know what that word means?"

"Yes, not all prostitutes are dumb, Mister. It means a disgrace, or an atrocity."

"Do you know what it's like growing up with this atrocity, and being subjective to bullying, the whispers behind your back, and even to your face?"

"No mister, I don't. Are you done talking yet?"

"Not quite. Do you know the beatings I endured because of something that was outside of my control?"

"Why didn't you just go to a dermatologist?"

"My mother refused. Her alcohol was more important than her son. She told me to suck it up."

"You're older now. Why don't you go now?"

"Good question. Recently, on impulse, I had called a dermatologist office. I explained to the woman on the phone my mustard discoloration along the left side of my body. She said I had two options. One would be a skin graft from another part of my body, and the other was laser treatment. She couldn't determine which one until she saw me. Both procedures sounded painful, and were out of my price range."

"I'm sorry, honey. I really am. I know this is your dime, but are we going to do anything today? You seem kind of nervous." She went closer to me. I could feel her breath in my face. "Do you have any fetishes? Want to suck my toes? Want me to suck your fingers? Some men's fetishes are role playing. Do you want me to be a nurse for you and take care of you?"

The electrical current I felt earlier short circuited. I felt deflated. "I feel like I owe you the truth. I am a virgin."

The hooker looked straight at me, and burst out laughing for a full thirty seconds. Every time her laughter subsided, she would look at me, and laugh again.

"What the hell is so funny?" I asked with anger.

She pointed at me. "Besides a prostitute, who would even think of screwing you?"

She went from compassionate to dispassionate quickly. "I don't find that funny."

That statement made her laugh even harder. "C'mon honey, let's do this, and get it over with!"

"Earlier you asked if I liked it fast or slow. I'm afraid you won't find out whether I like either one."

"Oh, really? Why, can't get it up? Beat off too much?"

Dear readers, I remained calm despite being angry and embarrassed. "No. While I poured my heart and soul to you, and told you I was a virgin, all you did was laugh at me, so I want to disclose something else I had left out."

"And what might that be, sugar? That you're gay? Transgender?"

"Again, no to all of the above. You see, you never asked me what I did for a living, and that will be your downfall. A client of mine has been looking for someone to surgically remove people's skin. That's what I do for money, and for the fun of it."

The woman started to laugh but saw I was serious. Flight or fight mode kicked in and she tried to run, but I caught her by her long brown hair, turned her around, and punched her in the face. She fell to the floor. I dragged her by her long dark hair and put her in between the two double beds so no one would be able to see what I was doing.

"Please don't kill me! I'll do anything you want!"

"I know you will!" I leaned down and punched her in her mouth. Blood trickled from her thick lips. I turned her over on her belly, and zip tipped her hands together. Then I re-positioned her on her back. I took a gander and liked her wide hips, just like I saw in some magazines at home.

The woman started to cry. I cried with her. Her tears were from outright terror; mine were derived from sheer delight. I rubbed her head like a puppy and hummed a melody to her. "You like that song? It was popular in the 1970's. You know it?" She shook her head no. "Really? How about if I hummed it again? Da Da... Dadada. Dowada do. No?" She shook her head no in fear. Her blue eyes bugged out.

I patted her tummy. "I just want you to know you're going to die tonight."

She was about to scream when I punched her in her face. I heard cartilage crack, and her nose had shifted to one side. "You broke my nose!"

I bent down to her, not too close where she could raise her head and bite me or head butt me, and said in a loving voice, "Yes, I did break your nose. Now shut the fuck up while I tell you a story." She tried to get up. I punched her in her belly, and she went limp. "Don't talk, don't try to get up. Just listen. Understand? Nod if you comprehend."

She slowly nodded, fear on her pretty face.

I stroked her beautiful long dark hair. "Believe it or not, it was true what I told you earlier. I have never been with a woman before." I removed her shirt and bra with my scissors, and put them in my garbage bag. Then, I removed her pants and panties. It was more difficult because her hands were zip tied behind her back, and she refused to help me. I was almost out of breath. "I am not undressing. I am going to make sure I leave no traces of me here. You, on the other hand, will have lots of traces left. My client only needs skin. I would prefer to take out your tendons, bones, and heart because you seem like a good specimen, but I do what the client wants, just like you, right?" She didn't respond, readers. Here I am being nice, trying to console her before I killed her, and she ignored me. Well, we couldn't have that, could we? I took her head and smashed it on the carpet a few times. Her eyes rolled in the back of her head. I had to slap her a few times to wake her up. "You're being uncooperative. Earlier you asked if I had a fetish. Mine is somewhat different than most people. Want to hear it?"

She shook her head no. "I just want to get home to my son."

I looked at her, and laughed. "If you even have a son, you'll never see him again. But back to what I was saying. Of course you want to hear my fetish, don't lie! I love bellies. I know you might think that's odd. I love a soft belly with a deep belly button. Weird, huh? The best part about that is your belly matches that description." I bent down and punched her stomach several times. She coughed. I thought she was going to throw up. "Feels good going all the way in, doesn't it?' I looked at her with disgust, and punched her again. "Perhaps it's best that I start the procedure now since you aren't interested in hearing anymore about my life's struggles. A shame, really." I grabbed my bag, took out a rag and the vial that contained the ether. Seeing the vial and rag brought a primal fear in the woman. She was about to scream when I punched her hard in her soft belly. Her eyes went wide with pain and she coughed. I took her face and forced her to smell the rag. She gagged and almost threw up. Finally, she fell unconscious. I carefully placed a sterile back table cover underneath her, put a back table cover on both beds, and took out my medical supplies. Then I carelessly threw her back on to her stomach, and cut the zip tie. I dragged her to the bed, hoisted her up, turned her around on her stomach again, took both of her arms, and zip tied them to the bed frame. Then I put my protective equipment on, and did the same procedure just like I did to the old man by shaving her back and legs, then cleansing the skin in circular motions. Unfortunately for her, she woke during the first pass of the dermatome surgically removing her skin. I had to force one of her socks in her mouth to prevent her from screaming. The noise of the dermatome was loud enough, but with her screaming, it would likely cause someone to call the police. It was then and there, dear readers that I realized something. I liked the person awake during the recovery process. I liked seeing the absolute terror in their pathetic eyes, and the way they convulsed when the dermatome made its first pass as the skin was being peeled off slowly. After I was finished I used soap, and washed her face. Now I could see her facial expression after I had removed her skin. She had passed out. I slapped her in the face hard several times. I heard a stirring. I punched her in her unprotected belly, because I liked it. I made sure I removed any trace of my presence by rolling her body off the back table covers, removed all of my personal protection equipment, and the ether rag. Then I put another pair of gloves on, rolled up the cover, and put it in a small garbage bag. Since she obviously wasn't dead yet, I could still see her chest rising, I took one of the pillows off the floor, put it on her mouth, and slowly suffocated her. It was interesting watching her gasp for breath until the light extinguished from her eyes. Now she was just an empty shell. Then, I carefully took all of my equipment with me and left.

It didn't end there, reader. Oh no. I went home, sat on my bed, and put my hand down my pants. I started to fantasize about the prostitute. I relived the way I showed her who the boss was. Stroking steadily, I increased my pace as I replayed the scenes in my head over and over. I ejaculated shortly thereafter. I felt like I was on top of the world!

February 9th

I was looking out my fourth story window between the vertical bars, and I saw snow falling heavily in all directions of McCordsville. The tree branches were hanging down from the weight. From afar, I could see snowmen on neighboring houses. Children were having snowball fights, and laughing. I had read the land the asylum was built one was once a gas station. The railroad tracks behind the building went through all of the small local towns. Even to this day, the trains ran at all times, waking me up during the night, and sometimes during my naps during the day. Meanwhile, the purity of the white snow falling steadily was in marked contrast to the dark feelings I was harboring. I glanced at my bent, crooked, and twisted hands, feeling hopeless. The outrage I felt at the orderly Steve, but in particular, the asshole Detective Jay Club, made me yell inwardly for what seemed like hours. I still vividly remember the conversations I had with the Detective. Since I possessed a photographic memory, I could recall them with clarity. I had bought a voice changer at a party store that made your voice sound metallic. After I skinned Arthur alive, and put him in the chair as though he was waiting for dinner, I had called Detective Jay Club. I called him specifically because I had read online he was assigned to the first case, which was Arthur Cooper. The investigation was still ongoing but I wanted to tell him about the new victim.

"Homicide," Jay growled into the phone.

"There's been a murder."

"Who? And where?"

I gave him the address, but I had noticed something. "You voice sounds deeper than your picture suggests, Jay."

"Hold on a second, pal. What's your name?"

"Never mind my name. I just told you there was a murder, and gave you the address."

"Why don't you come in and file an official report?"

Silly Detective. Did he really think I would fall for that, dear readers? "Hope you got some sleep, Jay, because there is going to be more murders. They say you need at least eight hours a day." See, I was trying to be nice.

"Cut to the chase. What do you want?" Jay said with callousness.

"Jay, that's no way to speak to someone who

could make or break your career. Here I am taking precious time out of my day to chat with you and all I receive is sarcasm."

"Again, what do you want?"

"See, there you go again. Well, Jay, I was thinking... I told you of one murder. That will definitely make you lose some sleep. Maybe you should get away for a while. Maybe relax a little, spend some time with your woman... oh, right. I forgot. You no longer have one. Sorry, Jay. Really, I am."

"Listen, you twisted son of a bitch! How the hell do you know about that?"

"Don't worry, Jay. It was in all the newspapers, remember? Anyway, I am here to help you. Don't be concerned. I've found you a woman. A very nice looking prostitute I picked out for you personally. Maybe you two could hook up and be friends... or friends with benefits. As luck would have it, I know a motel that will make you want to spend some time there. It's called Park Avenue Motel on the Westside of Indianapolis." I was trying to be friends with him. You know, help him out and do my civic duty by calling him about the murders I've committed. I figured since he was the one that was going to be coming after me, I should get to know him. But he wouldn't have it. All he did was to try to get me to come in, and talk to him. Wasn't that the purpose of the phone call? Some people! I hung up before he sent someone to trace my phone. I had more conversations with Detective Jay Club but found him to be an ass. Speaking of ass, I hear Mr. Orderly coming. I have to go. Until next time, dear readers.

February 17th

Something must be done with Steve, Mr. Orderly. I had made numerous complaints to the psychiatrist, Doctor Ellensworth, to no avail. Yesterday I was about to write in my journal when Mr. Orderly came in, and whacked my computer with his asp. The force of the impact cracked the top of my laptop. Luckily, I saw the light was still on. That meant it still worked. He looked at me and smiled broadly with his yellow stained teeth. He came toward me with the baton raised above his head, ready to strike me. He said, "I just heard from one of my rats you're writing a journal. I better not be in it. Am I in it, gnat?" I told him no. "What's your password?" I refused to tell him. I wet myself while he pretended to strike, then he would pretend to do it again and again. I was in no position to defend myself. "I better not be in your story or I will shove this baton so far up your ass they'll have to do surgery to remove it. And I'll make sure the anesthesiologist is detained so you'd be awake for the surgery." He laughed when he noticed my stained pants. Mr. Orderly then left, and I was left to try to change my pants and underwear. It is a difficult process when you barely have use of your hands.

March 2nd

Doctor Ellensworth was not a good psychiatrist. Despite the myriad of degrees that adorn her office walls, she still sucked. Her usual tactic was to tell me, when I told her repeatedly of the constant verbal and physical abuse that Mr. Orderly inflicted upon me is that he was not allowed to touch me. He could lose his job, and that I am making it up for the lack of attention I receive in here, versus being out in the real world and killing people. I think she's mad because the paper told everyone of our alleged affair. When I confronted her about the article, she recoiled.

"Never in a million years would I have an affair with anyone at work, especially an inmate, and an annoying one like you."

"Really?" I said. "What happened to being impartial and unbiased? The fucker is coming into my room, beating me with his baton, and verbally abusing me. Now, what the hell are you going to do about it?"

She started writing something in her damned notebook. I hated when she did that. She'd look up occasionally at me, shake her large head with her large bifocals, and then continued to write.

After a few minutes of uncomfortable silence, I yelled, "Will you stop writing in that stupid notebook!

What the fuck are you going to do about Mr. Orderly?"

She finally stopped writing. She looked at me with emotionless eyes. "Nothing. What I am going to do is prescribe you some medication."

I was astounded by her lack of compassion toward me. "Medicating me is your response? Surely you can't be serious! Haven't you heard one word I've confided to you?"

She sighed deeply. Doctor Ellensworth removed her spectacles, placed them on her bulky, messy, and unorganized desk. She rubbed her green eyes and said, "Steve is not the problem, you are, Ben. You are a social deviant. You contribute nothing to society. Impartiality is another name for indifference. I have to be indifferent which might seem biased to you, but believe me, I am not."

I felt my body tense. My shoulders stretched until I heard them crack like my knuckles use too before Detective Jay Club got hold of me. "You can spin your lies all you want with semantics, but the truth is you don't like me. Your hatred emanates from you. Your body exudes a total lack of respect which puts me in a precarious position. If you can't be objective, and I believe you can't, or won't, you need to step down."

I saw a flicker of something in her facial features. Was it revulsion? Disgust? Fear? She hastily regained her composure. "You have no authority over me. However, I have authority over you. I am prescribing some medication which may have some side effects, but rest assured, it's in your best interest to take them."

"What sort of side effects?" I remembered that cynical smile she gave me.

"They're nothing for you to worry about, Ben."

Famous last words. Dear readers, when someone tells you not to worry, that's when you worry. I left her office without any resolution. The solution to Mr. Orderly was obvious. He would need to die, but I couldn't do it with my ruined hands.

March 8th

It was a strange week, readers. Doctor Ellensworth ordered medication called Trazadone which, I found out, is primarily used for aiding in sleep. It was also used for major depression. I pretended to swallow the pill in front of Mr. Orderly. He liked to look in my mouth to make sure I ingested the pill. I hid it under my tongue. After a week of me pretending to be sedated, the madwoman psychiatrist stopped the prescription.

I could continue with the exploits of Doctor Ellensworth, and Mr. Orderly but I wanted to explain the process of taking grafts out of people, and how I chose them. I had received another email saying they were ready to have me take more than just skin. They wanted the lower extremity bones. I sent an email agreeing. Then I thought where would I find my next person? What better way to find potential victims than going to a mall? By that time, I had moved out of my mother's place, but the insane woman constantly called me. So, prior to going out to the mall, I had to placate my mom, and get her some food. I thought she had some in the fridge, and being somewhat of a good son, I went to her place and checked her kitchen. I almost vomited. Dishes with weeks of mold were piled up all over the kitchen. I opened up the cabinets, a swarm of flies dashed by me. Reluctantly I opened the fridge, and could not discern what was in there. I went to the sink and threw up whatever remains I had in my system. My mother was nearby watching. She called me pathetic and demanded that I buy her food and alcohol. She called me worthless, and several names before I wretched again. Finally, I told the old broad to shut the fuck up. That did the trick. She walked back to her chair, kicking liquor bottles that obscured her path, and sat down, took the remote, turned on some brainless show, and started cackling. God, I hated her laugh. I hated her too. I walked out of her house without uttering another word. One of these days I will get the last laugh. When I have her tied up, and cutting her open she'll cry. And when she cries out in pain, I will spit on her, and laugh. I'm sure none of her body parts were worth salvaging. Sorry readers, my mood is swinging toward hatred, and what good would that do when I relate to you my next victim I found at the mall? I will write when I am in a better frame of mind.

March 15th

Ah, the mall. What great pleasure I derived from watching the dredges of society gather. People were always in a hurry. They scuttle about as if the world was their oyster. They wore their fake clothing, make up, and displayed inappropriate behavior by flaunting their asses, or making sure their cleavage was within unacceptable parameters. Tweens taking selfies, macho men pretending the world trembled when they walked by you. All fake. The real people showed fear when they saw me, even when my hoodie overlapped my face, and wearing sunglasses. Almost all of my discoloration was hidden, but the mustard color was too pronounced not to hide all of it on my face. I chose a seat as far from the concession stand as I could. I nonchalantly looked around, seeking potential targets. I felt like the dominant male because I knew with certainty I could kill anyone here, and surgically remove almost any body part I wished. What power! Confidence coursed through my veins. I can vividly recall the supremacy I was feeling until I felt a presence near me. A woman had dared to sit down next to me! What the fuck? Leave! I yelled internally. You're ruining my moment of being King of the Hill! Still she sat there, defying me! I stole a quick glance at her. She had penetrating blue yes, slim figure (of what I could see since she had a fancy white jacket on), and a white hat with black strands of hair coming out on both sides.

"Hi."

She spoke to me! No one, and I mean no one, had ever spoken to me before. I always had to initiate the discourse. What do I do? What do I say?

"Sorry to intrude, but all the seats were taken."

She was so nice to me! Panic engulfed me. "That's... that's okay," I muttered. You idiot! The first time someone talked to you, and you gave them an answer where a response wasn't necessary. Then again, did I want to talk to this woman? What would become of the whole tidbits of conversation? Nothing. She'll see it was all a charade as soon as she got one look at my discoloration.

"Are you okay? You seem out of sorts."

Please stop talking to me. You're drawing attention to me. I wanted to scope out the place to kill, and here you are trying to engage in conversation. "Yeah, I'm fine."

After a moment of silence, she spoke again. "I see what's going on here," the woman said to me.

"Really? What's going on here?" I asked sarcastically. I didn't actually look straight at her, more to the right side where there wasn't any mustard color visible to her.

"You're checking out the women here. You're obviously single, a little disheveled, and wearing sunglasses so no one can trace your eye movements."

"What are you, a shrink?" I asked defensively.

She gave a soft laugh. "No, I am a nurse. I just got off from work, didn't feel like cooking, and this mall is on my way home. After a few years on the job, I can tell a lot about people."

"Really? What if I told you I was a serial killer, and a virgin? Would you believe me?"

She seemed taken aback, and then regained her composure. "I would tell you that you told me that for attention, and for shock value. And believe me, it worked!"

I let the conversation die out. I was thinking about getting up, and walking around. Talking to this girl would only lead to trouble. Trouble for her. I wanted to find someone a little less gregarious. Yes, someone less social, almost helpless looking. Then the bitch started talking again! Didn't she take the hint I did not want to talk to her?

"Hi, my name is Jen. Jen Walker."

She struck out her hand. I reluctantly accepted it, avoiding eye contact. "Ben. Ben Berstgel. What hospital do you work at?"

"Does it matter?"

"I guess not." It's at this point, dear readers, I was glad I had a photographic memory so I could record the absurd conversation that ensued.

"I've been dying to ask you a question, Ben."

Dying? We've known each other, what two minutes? Halfheartedly I said, "Oh? And what would that be?"

"I want you to remove your sunglasses, and take off your hoodie."

I looked at her as if she had lost her mind. "Are you fucking kidding me? Why the hell would I do that for? I don't even know you!"

"I want to see the real you not the person behind your jacket and sunglasses."

"No way. I don't know you, we're not friends!"

"What are you trying to hide, Ben?"

"And what concern of that is yours? What are you trying to hide?"

"Nothing, I am just curious. I want to see you for who you really are."

"What you see is what you get. Now, get off my back!"

Jen looked at me as if she was debating whether or not to continue with the conversation. Don't Jen, just don't.

"Why are you trying to deliberately end this talk? I'm trying to be friendly, and just wanted to know what you're hiding."

"I am not hiding anything. This conversation is done. I'm leaving!" I stood up; clearly thinking she would stay, and let me leave. Nope, she got up from the table as I rose. Typically I am a very shy person, don't like confrontations, and just want to be left alone. Evidently this nurse, Jen Walker, was trying my patience. "What are you doing?"

"What do you mean, Ben?"

"Why did you get up when I did?"

"Obviously you don't want my friendship, so I am going home."

"You set a condition I am unwillingly to make to attain that friendship."

"By asking you to reveal your true self?" she said incredulously.

"Yes! And to make matters worse, you wanted me to do it in front of all these people!"

Jen let out a heavy sigh. "I'm sorry. I didn't think it was a big deal. I encounter people with deformities everyday where I work."

I became livid, and shouted at her. "I am not deformed!" Oops. People turned to stare at our heated exchange. I turned and walked away. I felt her walking behind me. I wasn't sure if she was walking my way because her car was parked in the direction I was walking, or she was following me. I turned down the corridor that led to a large department store. I had parked my beat up hunter green 2010 Chevy Impala in their parking lot. I had parked all the way in the back where there was less light. It sucked I had to hide the stain on my body because of peoples' prejudices. It would have made my life a hell of a lot easier, and probably would not have led me to the place in life I am in currently. I stole a glance behind me. Jen was marching fast behind me. She caught up to me and grabbed my hand. I saw the veins protrude, which meant she was using some exertion to stop me. Was this woman crazy? Did she really want to die? On any other occasion, I would have gladly let her manhandle me, and then show her what it was like to be manhandled back. But this woman, this nurse Jen Walker, had done what no other person had ever done before. She talked to me. I guess I owed her that much to stop, and listen to her. I slowed down, and then stopped. We were in the middle of the hallway, right in front of a department store. The overhead illumination was too bright. She would be able to see my tainted left side much more clearly. I panicked. Do I stay here, or tell her to go somewhere where it darker? Would that sound weird? Fuck it. I motioned her to go into the department store. She seemed to think it over before she nodded her assent. I walked in front of her, and brought her to the darkest place I could find. I stopped, and she almost fell into me. It was a weird feeling. I could feel her breasts against my back. I quickly shook that from my mind.

"Look Ben, I just wanted to apologize. It was an insensitive thing to say."

Chalk one up to the politically correct atmosphere that still permeates society. "That's okay. I'm used to people being tactless, and inconsiderate."

"Hey, I'm trying to apologize here. You don't have to be a dick about it."

She did have a point. A small, smidgen, tiny, morsel of a point despite what I said was true. "Sorry," I said meekly.

Jen smiled. "Apology accepted!"

"Jen Walker, I now have a question for you."

She looked at me. Her white jacket was overshadowed by her blue eyes. "Yes?"

"Why are you being so nice to me?"

"I am a floor nurse. I meet people all the time that are lonely, or are in need of a friend. You seemed the type."

"Are you always upfront with them?"

"No, not usually. But something was amiss with you. I couldn't place it until I saw you from afar, and thought, gee, that guy could use a friend. Now I see what is... muddled about you. You are obviously hiding your face and perhaps your body too. Did you get burned when you were younger?"

"NO! I did not get burned. Are you feeling sorry for me? Is that what this is about? I don't need your sympathy!" I saw people looking at our exchange as they walked by us.

"Relax, Ben! Look, let's not talk here. You seem to get uptight really quick. I don't usually do this, but did you want to go out to a bar and have a drink?"

"Thank you, but I don't drink."

"How about going to my place? Just to talk!" She emphasized that pretty quick by putting up her hands.

"Um, are you sure?" Excitement surfaced. I can pretend to be her friend, and then kill her. I could take a lot of body parts. I wouldn't take her veins. Women's veins tend to be smaller and more narrow then men's.

"Yes, I'm a sucker for hard cases. No offense."

"None taken. Where are you parked?"

"I am parked behind this department store. Where are you parked?"

"Same." We walked to her car in silence. She unlocked her semi-new Ford Focus and got in. I pointed to a row far removed from everyone. "I am parked over there. Wait for me, and I will follow you." She nodded. I jogged to my car, got in, started it, and saw my medical bag on the front passenger floor. We'll see how this night goes, whether or not I would take some of her body parts. That thought thrilled me!

I drove behind her, making sure I didn't get too close. My stomach had butterflies. She turned left out of the mall in Indianapolis, and went east on 82nd street. I remembered we passed several lights, a made a left on Craig street. We went a couple of miles, made a right, then a quick right into a townhouse addition. She parked and pointed to a spot right beside her. I parked and looked at my medical bag. We were parked under a street light, so I opted not to grab it in case people were looking at us. Paranoid? Sure, but I wanted to kill her. I won't be stupid enough to come out of her house with all sorts of garbage bags, and quite possibly her entrails and blood that I wouldn't want to clean up. Nope, too messy here. Have to lure here somewhere else. Tonight, I'll pretend to be her friend, and meet someplace more rural and secluded. I sighed deeply, reluctantly got out, and met her at her door.

We walked straight in. To my left was a tiny kitchen. In front of me was a vast living room, dining room combo. To my right was a door that was slightly ajar. I looked in. It was a half bath. The wallpaper was decorated with a wide assortment of cats. Beyond that there was a staircase which, I presumed, led upstairs to the bedrooms. I glimpsed a small baseball bat with a couple of umbrellas in a ceramic pot not two feet away from me.

"Why do you have a kid's size baseball bat? You have kids?" That would be a major bummer if I had to deal with her heathens too.

She gave a light laugh. "No, that's for protection. The larger bats are too bulky and heavy."

I nodded, pretending I wasn't interested anymore. But actually, I was. An idea surfaced. I walked all the way to the end of the room where the drawn blinds were. Behind the large free flowing blinds, a sliding glass door stood. I parted the blinds. Total darkness. I could barely discern her neighbors. There was a tradeoff. Yes, I could surgically remove her skin, and de-bone her here, and sneak out the back. But there was too much light in the front. Somehow, I would have to get rid of the lights out front but that presented another problem. I wasn't sure if there were any cameras out front. Come to think of it, the more I thought of doing her here, the less likely the idea seemed.

Jen took her jacket off. She was wearing a light blue sweater that resembled a turtleneck, only thicker. Her jeans were tight. She looked at me expectantly. "Aren't you going to take off your jacket, and that silly hoodie?"

"Look Jen, there's something that you should know about me."

Her eyes gleaned. "Yeah, you told me already. You're a serial killer, and a virgin. I get it, you're shy."

I kept my hoodie well beyond my face to cover the stain. Yeah, that's a good word to describe it. "No,

I was just joking about that." Readers, I really wasn't joking but why tell her that? "I was born with a discoloration on my left side from my head all the way down to my toes."

"I knew there was something. I had caught glimpses of a different color skin. However, you seem quite adept at hiding it with your hood. But hey! I'm a nurse. Do you know how many people I see with different... abnormalities? I can handle it. Just show me."

Good lord folks, I actually considered it! Before my hands got two inches from my side, I scrambled to the bathroom, and locked the door. I took the hoodie and sunglasses off, and stared into the mirror, and saw a person I loathed. Why, oh why, did god give me this stain? I traced my face where the two different colors met, and let out a slight whimper. I refused to cry here. At my house crying was fine. But in front of this nurse, Jen Walker? Never. I heard tentative knocking on the door.

"Are you okay, Ben?"

I wiped the sole tear that had somehow managed to escape. "Yes, I'm fine. I am building up the courage to show you my true self."

"Why would that take courage?"

Has she not heard anything I told her? Jesus Jen, what the hell? That bat looked like the only friend I have here tonight. "Jen, I don't typically show anyone my shortcomings. Give me a sec, will ya?"

"Take your time," she mumbled as her voice receded.

Okay. I thought about this logically. Why not show her my mustardness? After all, I'm going to skin and de-bone her eventually. I have been fearful of showing her all this time, what silliness! Rationalization can do wonders to the human psyche. To error on the side of caution, I opted to put the sunglasses and hood back on. I gave a few deep breaths, and opened the door. I took deliberate and measured steps toward the living room. Jen was on the couch, facing away from me. She had turned on her huge television. I noticed wireless speakers around the room. Huh, surround sound. Damn, it would be so easy for the kill right now. If only those streetlights weren't so bright! And who knew if there were cameras? I sat on the other side of the sofa.

"You know, you shouldn't wear the hoodie, sunglasses and any other attire to hide your true self."

What the hell did she know? To humor her I asked, "Really, and why is that?"

"Because you're trying to hide what you really look like. But by hiding your discolored skin, you stick out. Counterproductive, Ben."

So now Jen is a nurse and a fucking psychologist? I peered over to the baseball bat. The bat started talking to me. "Ben, you know you want to bludgeon her. Take me, and stop thinking about it, and do it!" Now readers, at this point you would say I was insane. Inanimate objects like bats don't talk. They can't. But, I would be willing to take a lie detector test, and it would prove I was telling the truth. I ignored the bat, and concentrated on Jen. "What's counterproductive is this conversation. Actually, it's inane."

Jen's blue eyes bore through me, and completely ignored my previous statement. "By wearing what you're currently wearing, or a ski mask, or anything that hides your features, people will stay away from you."

"Good. That's the plan." That's when the bat whispered to me, "Ben, take me, hit her on her damned head, and get this silly conversation over with. I am getting restless." I looked to Jen. It seemed she hadn't heard the bat talk. Good, it would be the bat and my little secret.

"That is a terrible plan, Ben. Why do you think no one sat at your table in the mall?"

Jesus Jen, stop talking. You don't know how close I am to getting my medical kit out of my car, and to hell with the consequences. "No one sat with me because I was all the way in the back."

Jen gave a deep sigh. I think she was giving up on me. The feeling was mutual. Chalk it up to lost causes. "Yes, of course you were sitting way in the back. However, once people saw you with your attire, their preconceived judgment kicked in. Look Ben, television show and movies depict people dressed like you, more often than not, as the bad guys. The perception of make believe bleeds into real life."

Dear reader, Jen used an interesting word choice, bleed. I don't give a shit if television or the movies portrayed masks, or hoodies as being bad, and bled into the real world. I don't care if someone bled figuratively, like Jen's analogy, or literally bleeds because I am *blind to blood* on both accounts. I have had enough of Jen's critique of societal norms, and what I should do. What I should do is take my friend the bat or a knife in the kitchen, anything to terminate her punishing discourse. Before I did anything, I needed to learn something. "You have an interesting point. I will think about it. Can we change the subject, please?"

She nodded her approval.

"How long have you lived here?"

"Seven years."

"I noticed a dumpster. Is that where residents dump their garbage?"

"Duh, yes, everyone knows that."

I bit my tongue on her sarcastic response. "What about people from outside the complex that dump their mattress, or any other stuff the garbage men won't take?"

"That is a problem since the property managers won't spend the money on outside cameras."

Bingo. It was then a realization struck me. Had I started with that sentence, none of the pointless conversation would have taken place. Well dear readers, my voice is starting to break from relating my story. I will continue on another day. I know you want to know what happened with Jen Walker, but I am not in good health. My voice is cracking.

March 16th

It took me a full day for my voice to recuperate. I don't talk to many people where I reside, and talking into the microphone strained my voice. Well, time to resume where I had left off. Once Jen told me there were no cameras outside, my two obstacles were the light in the front of the complex, and my car. People wouldn't necessary look at my car, but once the death of Jen Walker became known, people would remember a vehicle that wasn't usually parked here. That was a rookie mistake on my part, dear readers. One I had to rectify. I could take out the streetlight easily enough, but my car was the problem. Damn, how stupid I was to bring my car here. I should have feigned car trouble. It was then I made the final decision not to kill her here because I kept vacillating. I had to meet her somewhere more reclusive. We were still on the couch while I was thinking the scenario through. I would unquestionably get caught. So, Jen would live another day. "Jen, I am getting a migraine. I am going to have to leave. However, I enjoyed our talk so much; I was wondering if we could do it again soon?" It was a lie, but I had to sound sincere.

"Sure. Do you want my cell number?"

Folks, I couldn't do that. If I had her number on my cell, and something happened to her, the police would trace me through her contact list. "I accidentally left my phone at home."

"I've done that plenty of times! How about I just write my number down, and give it to you?"

"Or you could just meet me somewhere to talk?"

"You don't want my number?" She asked in confusion.

"Of course, I do. It's just I don't want to call you at work. Being a floor nurse, I would imagine it would be difficult for you to talk." Wow, I made that one up on the fly.

"You're right, hadn't thought of that. Okay, where, and when?"

Hmm, I didn't think this all the way through. What was close enough to my house where I could walk to, but far enough not to attract any attention? There was a Sandy Pantry convenience store about two miles from my house, but once we got there, how would I lure her back to my house without her vehicle, and without being seen? *Damn, why does luring people to their deaths have to be so difficult?* Then I remembered a short cut through the woods. It was dense, a half an acre or so, and had an old shack that was abandoned. Usually kids hung out there and drank, smoked pot, and whatever kids did these days. I would have to make sure the shack didn't house any people, hide my medical stuff there, and convince her to walk home with me. Readers, what about her car? I couldn't siphon the gas, or put a thin slice in her brake line because people would see me tinkering with her car. Then another thought popped into my head. There's a dive bar a half a block down the road with very little illumination with a large parking lot. I'll meet her there, and then somehow convince her to walk to my house, take a shortcut through the woods, and then kill her in the shack. I am a fucking genius.

"Today is Thursday. How about we meet on Saturday about nine pm at the bar called Jerseys?"

"Sure, I know where that's located. Say, I forgot to ask you something. What do you do for a living?"

"I work as a receiving clerk at a Jake's hardware store."

"Of course, out of the public eye."

I had no compunction about lying to her. It was those snide remarks she kept making which would make it easier for me to terminate her existence. "Yeah, something like that. Man, my head is pounding. I'll see you Saturday."

"Bye, Ben."

My head wasn't pounding. I felt great, exhilarated even. I left her house in high spirits. I just had to get through one more day at work, and the beauty of it was I wasn't on call this weekend so I could take my time extracting her skin, and de-boning her. Life was good, readers. Life was good.

March 18th

Dear readers, I could not quell the excitement I was feeling. Jen Walker would suffer greatly tonight. While she was probably the only friend I ever had, she had to go. I will not lie. I de-skinned and de-boned people for a living. But outside of my regular job I did it for profit, and also for fun. All of my careful planning led me to where I was now. I walked the two plus miles in the still chilly mid-March weather. I chose a path which had the least lighting, coupled with my over-sized dark attire, including the hoodie, made me almost invisible to people. Prior to arriving here, I made sure the shack was semi-clean, and had no inhabitants. I didn't know what I would have done if there was anyone there, but luck was on my side tonight. I checked my watch. It was two minutes before nine when I saw Jen pull in the parking lot. I motioned her to where I was, all the way in the back. She parked without hesitation near where I stood. I wondered, as she pulled alongside me, what thoughts would rage in her mind, if she knew this would be her last day on planet earth. She got out of her car and locked her door remotely. She was wearing a green jacket with an attached fluffy hood, white gloves, and a white hat with different colored cats that went all around. She had a green handbag that was slung around her slender shoulders.

I wore a heavy black jacket, a hoodie, and thin

pair of black driving gloves. And of course my sunglasses even though it was in the evening.

She looked around the parking lot. "Where's your car?"

"Car trouble, it wouldn't start."

"You didn't walk all the way here, did you? Do you live far?"

Again with the fucking questions. "I live about two miles from here."

"Did you want to go in to the bar?"

This is where I would have to convince her to *walk* home with me. "I was thinking of a change of venue."

"I thought it was odd you wanted to meet me at a bar when you told me you don't drink."

Shit, forgot about that. She's too perceptive. I decided to change the subject. "Did you tell all of your friends you were meeting a guy tonight?" I tried to sound like I didn't care, but I really did.

She laughed. "No, it's not like we're dating. We're just friends. And I wanted to see what you really look like under your facade."

I could take that statement a few ways but decided to leave it alone. I was happy she didn't tell a soul. "I have an odd request, Jen."

"You? An odd request? Who would have thunk?"

I wanted to bitch slap here right there, but good things happen to those who wait. "Since we are "friends", I was wondering if you would take a walk with me to my house, chat, and get to know each other better."

"You want me to walk two miles?"

One good thing came from that statement. She didn't add, *and to your house*? "Normally I would say yes. I walked the two miles here to clear my head. But I know a short cut through the woods that would shave a mile off it, if you want. If you don't want to walk, I would perfectly understand." It was a gamble but one I was more than willing to make.

Jen looked around, then took a good hard look at me, and shrugged. "Yeah sure, why not? What could it hurt? I need the exercise anyway."

Wow, this was going a lot smoother than I thought. "Great, follow me. The woods are only about a quarter of a mile from here. It will be smooth sailing after that."

"Lead the way."

I started walking but found I was going too fast for her. In my line of work, I had to walk fast. Since I didn't want to seem eager, I slowed my pace. Soon we were side by side.

"It's pretty out this way. With my work schedule, I don't get a chance to get out much," Jen said as I saw her breath.

I was going to be kind to her, even if it killed me. Get the irony, folks? "Yeah, I don't get out much either, but it's not because of work."

"What do you do when you're not working, Ben?"

"I like to read."

"Any specific genres?"

"Nope, like them all. Does your boyfriend like to read?"

"I don't currently have a boyfriend."

I was surprised. "That means you did at one time. What's his name?"

She stopped dead in her tracks. "I don't want to

discuss him."

I stopped too, and put up a hand. "Wait a second, you want me to open up, and remove my hoodie, which is a monumental step for me, and you won't discuss your ex? That doesn't make any sense, Jen."

She looked at me for the briefest of moments. "Okay, he's a nurse in the surgery department where I work."

"Where did you guys meet?" A scheme was forming in my mind as we started to walk again.

"We met in the cafeteria. We sat together because we had a mutual friend."

What was your ex-boyfriends name?"

"A.J Mandery. We don't speak anymore."

"Why, what happened between you two lovebirds?"

"He... he liked to be too rough in the sack."

"Didn't like that, huh? Did he tie you up?"

"He wanted to but I wouldn't allow it. He did other things which I won't speak about. Suffice to say, we don't speak. I don't really care for him."

"Has he threatened you?"

"Why? Are you going to go after him, and defend my honor?"

Is she for real? "Uh, no. Not a fighter. Not a lover. I am nothing. But, getting back to the subject, you don't like him, is the feeling mutual?"

She laughed. "Oh yes! He doesn't like me at all! We had a really bad breakup. He told me he better not see me outside of work, or I would know what rough was really like."

Good, I could use that, if need be. I didn't respond. We changed the subject and chatted about superficial topics. I was trying really hard to keep up with the conversation but my heart was beating fast. It was jumping up and down with joy. Finally, I saw the shack. How to convince her to go inside? Seemed I didn't have to.

"How about we take a break from walking, and rest in the shack, Ben? I'm tired."

Floor nurses. You'd think they were up for a walk since they're on their feet all day! "Good idea. I need to rest too. I walked all the way to the bar, and now here." I wasn't tired, but my response fit with the situation, dear readers.

We got to the door, I motioned her to go first, and then I walked in. It was small, about twenty-five feet by twenty- five feet. The moon allowed us to see inside while the door was ajar. A small fireplace was on the back wall. The bricks were cracked, and some were strewn haphazardly across the floor. A well-used mattress was to the right, and to the left was a recliner with a blanket covering it. To the side of the chair was a small yellowed love seat that had been beaten down by excessive use. My medical kit, and ancillary stuff, was perched behind the chair, outside of Jen's prying eyes. Luckily, I had brought a generator so I could have electricity in this diminutive building to plug in the dermatome.

I closed the door to total darkness. I rehearsed where the furniture was, found the several candles I placed there, and lit them. Prior to coming here, I also had shut the two windows and put up old, dusty blankets I had found here. And yes, I used gloves so no traces of my fingerprints were here. And really, who the hell would want to touch any of the nasty stuff in here?

"You always keep candles in out of the way shacks, Ben?" Jen asked in the pitch blackness.

Think fast, Ben. "In this particular one, yes. I often walked to Sandy Pantry to clear my mind. Sometimes I take the time to come in here at night after an exhaustive day at work. I brought candles so the place would have some light, but not too much. There is power here; I have tried the switch before people stole the lamps. During the daylight, you can see the power lines that come to the roof." Power lines weren't working, however my generator was, but I wasn't telling her that. I lit the candles and the illumination was too much on the romantic side, something I wasn't feeling, and I was sure Jen wasn't either.

My response seemed to work. She changed the subject. "Shall we sit down and rest, Ben?"

"You want to sit down on the love seat? I don't know what is crawling on it, or whose been on it doing you know what."

"Just until we rest a little, Ben. C'mon, you scared? I thought you came here often to think."

Actually, I was scared. God knows what people had done on the love seat, but I could also wash my clothes after I procure her body parts. "Okay, I'll sit. When I come here, I usually bring a clean blanket, and sit on the floor." She made no room for me. I had to sit right next to her. We sat in silence for a second.

"Actually, Ben I have a confession to make."

I was going to say something along similar lines to get the killing done quickly. "Oh? What's that?" I felt something being pushed into my ribs. What the hell was that?

She leaned in close to me. The pain in my ribs increased. "I know who you are."

Readers, imagine my surprise. How could she possibly know who I am? I've only killed two people, my father and a prostitute. She, if I didn't die first, would be my third. Inwardly I panicked. "Okay, who am I?" I asked with as much innocence as I could muster.

"You murdered the old man, and the prostitute." The pressure was removed from my ribs. I was now staring at a 380. Looked like a Smith & Wesson with a small grip.

I laughed to try to control the tense situation. "Really? How did I do that?"

"Please don't give me the sob story of you being a receiving clerk. I checked out your fairy-tale story. I went to the store you supposedly worked at. No one ever heard of you. When I found out how the two innocent people were killed by surgically removing their skin, I did further research. Surgeons could do it, but my instinct told me you weren't a doctor of any type."

"Thanks?"

"Oh, don't get me wrong. You're intelligent, and cunning."

"So, what made you suspicious?"

"You're admitting to these crimes?"

"Not in the slightest. I never killed anyone."

"Can I continue so we can stop this charade you're putting on? Thank you. I became suspicious because of how you were dressed, it made you stick out. I was trying to warn you earlier when I told you my opinion. The way you hid in the background, the attire you chose to wear, and the way you watched people."

"That doesn't make me a killer. You observations are hardly a basis for anything. It's all conjecture and baseless." I heard a click.

"That noise you just heard was me removing the safety. While my previous statements are supposition, I followed you Thursday after you left my house. Found out where you live, then followed you to your work the next morning. You work at an Organ harvesting company."

"I don't work for an Organ harvesting company."

She put the gun up to my face. "Liar!"

"I remove tissue, not Organs."

"It's the same thing!" She put both hands on the grip of the gun, and steadied herself.

"No, it's not. There is a big difference between Organ, tissue, and eye removal. Organs are removed when the person is still alive, albeit they are brain dead, or from CTOD, or cardiac time of death. Tissue and eyes are removed once the person has expired, and each graft has a certain amount of time before the graft is no longer viable."

"But you removed the skin. That's the biggest Organ in the body."

"We remove skin, and we remove the heart, both are considered Organs while they're alive. When they're dead, they are considered tissue."

"I'll take your word for it. I want to know more."

"Why? Are you really a nurse?"

"Yes, I am a floor nurse. But my uncle is a Detective. I grew up around law enforcement. As soon as I learn all I can from you, I am going to call my uncle, and have you arrested."

I faced her. "You're not going to anything of the kind, and I am not telling you anything more. Now I know why you were so accommodating. Even walking to the shack, you were going to confront me."

"And what were you going to do to me? Skin me alive?"

What the hell? I might as well tell her. "Yes, and de-bone you too. I was considering other body parts but my client only wants your skin and your lower bones. Nothing personal, Jen. But back to the tissue topic. Normally we would have to find out if you were a viable candidate or not by asking your next of kin over fifty questions. If you had cancer within five years, were you in a certain country between these years, etc. And of course, we would have to take blood from your subclavian. One time I couldn't extract blood from a donor, so I had to go directly into the heart. No blood, no recovery."

"Really, you're going to remove my body parts? How? Where? Do you plan on doing it in this small, dimly lit shack?"

"Yes, but I'm not taking any blood from you, or asking you any prior medical history questions."

"Why not? Isn't that a requirement?"

"So calm and confident with that gun, aren't ya, Jen? Yes, it is. But in the case of the old man, the prostitute, and you, I don't really give a shit about your medical history. And apparently, the client I work for doesn't either. And truth be told, I have my medical kit and equipment behind the chair." I pointed to the chair. When she took her eyes off me, and looked at the spot I was pointing toward, it gave ample time for me to punch her squarely in the nose. The gun flew out of her hand as she fell down on her back on the love seat. I punched her repeatedly in her face until there wasn't any movement. I rushed to my bag, retrieved all of the supplies, and then ran back to the couch. I put a couple of sterile back table covers on the floor, and threw Jen carelessly on to her back. She groaned, which pleased me. A thought popped into my mind. Since she and A.J. disliked either other intensely, why not take her gun, and find out where he lived, and put it somewhere where the police would find it. I quickly put on another pair of gloves, and carefully put it in a small plastic bag. Hurriedly I put on my personal protective equipment, took off the pair of sterile gloves, and put on three pairs of sterile gloves. I removed all of her clothing, and put them in a garbage bag. I put her on her back. She tried to get up. I took the front of her head and slammed it on the ground a few times. That did the trick. I looked down and punched her in her belly because I wanted to. Because I liked to. I looked her skin over. I should get three square feet regardless. That's the least amount the client wanted. I have already explained how to remove people's skin, so I won't be redundant, dear readers. After I completed taking her skin, I took Jen's hair, pulled up her head, and slapped her across her face a few times. "Hey Jen, you awake?" No response. I slapped her harder, and she stirred awake. "Hey Jen, guess your plan didn't go the way you wanted it to."

"I... I... called... my... uncle. He'll... be... here... shortly..."

"I don't believe you. He would be here by now, especially since you had your suspicion about me. You would have had him meet you here. I'll have to do some investigation of my own to see if you lied about your uncle being a detective." I let go of her head and her face hit the back table cover.

So readers, you want to know what I did next? Of course you do! I had to take her lower bones! Jen was already sterile and prepped because I had shaved her legs, and cleaned them with the liquid soap. I got my sterile scalpel blade, and starting on her left side of her left leg, I cut the initial incision four inches above her hip bone, made sure the blade was superficial (close) to the skin, and cut down her skin slowly in the middle of her left leg. I looked at Jen. She wasn't doing too well. I slapped her hard in her face to get the grimace off her face. Damn, Jen! Die with some dignity, will ya! Resuming, I moved the blade toward the inner thigh, and went behind the patella, or the kneecap, then carefully, because Jen's skin was tight in that area, moved the blade more superficial, or closer, to the skin because I didn't want to cut any of the anterior tibialis, which is located at the calf. I looked to see if she was still breathing. She was. She was probably in a great deal of pain! You would not believe the euphoria I was feeling now, dear readers!

I started to peel back the skin. I put a new sterile scalpel blade under her skin, but above the adipose (yellow fatty deposits directly under the skin), to help speed up the peeling process. Her skin was now in half. One flap of skin was on one side of her left leg, the other flap was on the other side, close to her right leg, but not too close to compromise sterility. That may sound gross to some of you, dear readers, but not to me! I considered it a work of art. Now the entire left leg had skin on both sides, peeled, and I saw Jen's adipose all over her left leg. Right under the adipose, the fascia (a thin membrane covering the muscle or tissue) was mine for the taking. I had to be careful or I would cut into the muscle. I cut along the lines of the exposed fascia, careful not to take the tissue, and carefully removed it. I placed that in a sterile container where I had marked the top with fascia. It's always good to have the containers for the grafts marked prior to a recovery, dear readers. It saves time. The next graft to take was the Gracilis tendon. I had to cut her Sartorius tendon to get to the Gracilis and the Semitendinosus tendon. (Readers, if you spread out your hands on your inner thigh from slightly below your crotch to your kneecaps, the tendons I am explaining how to remove are located underneath that area). I cut, and peeled off the Satroius tendon, which was on top of the Gracilis and the Semitendinosus when I heard Jen gasp. I smiled as I took firm hold of the Gracilis tendon, felt where it started, and where it ended, then cut the tendon as far down as possible, then cut the connective tissue which was attached to the Garcilis. I looked over at Jen. He face was all scrunched up, with her eyes closed in pain, her forehead creased with wrinkles. A smile spread across the expanse of my face. There's nothing quite like removing body parts on people who were still alive!

I came out of my daydream. I used sterile wrapping paper, wrapped it, and wrote the name of the graft with my sterile marker, then took off another pair of sterile gloves, and donned three more sterile gloves. Now, it was the Semitendinosus tendon turn. This one was big. Again I found where the graft started and ended and sliced as much as I could, removed it, and did the same thing by marking it.

Now dear readers, by this time you would think

Jen Walker were dead. But her resiliency astounded me. Her breath came in small gasps, but damn she was still with me. She was probably beyond any pain a mortal could feel. I almost felt sorry for her. Almost.

While I was at it, I might as well take her Anterior & Posterior Tibialis. The Anterior Tibialis started from close to the kneecap, and ran down over the ankle bone. I went as far proximal (upper part) as I could, located it, and cut the tendon. I heard a short puff of air from Jen, then nothing. She had died bravely. I briefly thought whether or not AJ Mandery would miss her. It was the Anterior Tibialis that did her in. Not feeling sorry for her, I took the graft I had just cut, and pried and peeled it loose, all the way to the ankle bone. I reached behind the bone, found the distal (lower part) most portion of the tendon, and then cut it. I wrapped it, and marked it left Anterior Tibialis. The Posterior Tibialis tendon ran from the tibia (shin bone) down near the toes. I got as much as I could by pulling the tendon without ripping it, and cut as far as I could both distal (lower) and proximal (upper). I marked them accordingly. I did the same for the grafts on other side. I decided not to take her Humerus, Radius, and Ulna (all of the bones that make up the arms) because of time constraints, and because the client didn't want me to. I looked at her nude form, then at her arms. She hardly had any flab. Good for you, Jen! God, how I wanted to take her arm bones out! But, I still had to take out her lower bones. I went to the uppermost point of the femur (thigh bone), with its head perched in the Acetabulum (the socket that keeps the femur in place at the hip). I cut away the muscle that was attached and surrounded the thigh bone. Going higher, I went to where the femur head met the Acetabulum, and cut the ligament that connected them. Then I went lower to where the thigh bone met the kneecap and sliced it through the ligament, and I removed the thighbone. Whew! Dear readers, my voice is getting hoarse explaining the process! Hopefully you're able to follow alongside me! I looked at poor Jen. Her eyes were open, and she was staring at the ceiling.

I had to take the time to wrap the femur in a large clear bag, and then wrap it in thick blue wrapping paper. It's not the wrapping paper for gifts, it a wrapping paper for grafts. After that, I found where the tibia and fibula met (both at the top of the knee and down near the ankle, readers). I had to cut away the tissue, or the meat, to be able to see the bones. (See how awesome the recovery process is?) I separated them using a blade and careful exertion. I had a bag labeled for each side of the leg and what graft it was. I did the same for the other side too. Then, of course, it was the Achilles tendon next. One thing I never understood, readers. The Achilles tendon was attached to the Calcaneus (heel) bone, yet the tissue company considered it a tendon, not a bone. But since it was the lowest part of the body, I did it last. Folks, you had to be careful with the Achilles tendon, and make sure you cut up as far as you can with the muscle. Next, it was time to take out the hip bone. It was at the initial cut line four inched above the hip. I had to dig out the flesh with the scalpel blade to feel my way inside her body. When the area was wide enough, I went inside and used a metal chisel and mallet, and hammered it until the bone separated, then went inside her body, twisted and turned the bone until I heard it snap. The snapping part of the bone was my favorite part. You knew you had it; you had to make certain you didn't damage the iliac crest. And that bone is sharp! One time I took a crest out, and the bone was so pointy, it brushed up against my right hand, and punctured my sterile glove!

I retrieved the hip bone from her other side. Jen had good crests. You have to do the crest bone last because it's right below the bowels. You cut too high and hit the bowels, it contaminated everything. And it stunk to high heaven if it was punctured, believe me I know. I've smelled it when one of the techs accidentally went too far up, and cut it. Then, if the donor is of age, you could take out his or her peritoneal membrane, which is the lining that holds your intestines in place. I could also take her heart and pericardium. But that's for another day. Suffice to say, I had a lot of clean up to do to make it look like no one was here. And, again, here is where I deviate from the norm, folks. After a typical recovery, I used PCV pipes that were made at the office, and put them where the bones and tendons used to be. The larger size PCV pipe was to replace the leg bones that were removed, and the smaller ones were for the arms so the person looked more presentable at the funeral. The tissue place had bottles of powder that you poured inside the boneless legs, and if applicable, the arms. It absorbed the blood and edema (internal body liquid) that came with removing body parts. I decided not to do that with any of the people I have, or will, kill outside of work. I donned another pair of gloves, it no longer had to be sterile because the recovery was over, and everything was wrapped. But all I had were sterile gloves. I looked in my large medical bag, and found the thick, white suture. I made sure I purloined the suture that had wax on it from the tissue place so when I sutured Jen's body up, it would be easier for the long S shaped needle to penetrate Jen's skin. See? I thought about Jen in a good way. I used a loose stitch and sutured what was called a baseball stitch. One stitch over the other one. I used a loose stitch meaning I didn't put the stitches close together. That would have been a tight stitch, readers. Jen's lower body looked like it had been through an autopsy. Funeral directors differed on what type of stitching they preferred so usually either me, the other tech, or the circulator would ask him what type of stitching they preferred. I came out of my reverie, looked at my bloody gown, and smiled. Now I had to think of a place to dispose of her body. I took off my bloodied gown, and tossed it in the garbage bag and put a clean one on. She'll be missed in a few days, at the latest. I got all of my body parts in a cooler with ice. Then I wrapped up poor Jen Walker using the back table covers I had under her, and next to her. I tied the bags with rope I brought with me. My house was about a mile away and the damned cooler was heavy, not to mention Jen's body, even though half her weight had been removed. I hoisted the cooler, and placed it outside, behind the shack. Once I was done here, I had to drive to an undisclosed location once I texted a number that, I was told, was untraceable. But where do I put Jen's body? I heaved her body slowly outside the shack. I went back inside and blew out the candles. I smashed them against the back wall, and the candle glass shattered. I uprooted the couch, and chair. Basically, I tried to make it look like the place had been ransacked, folks. I didn't have a shovel, and I decided right there and then that I was not, was not, going to drag her damned body all over creation. Screw it, I dragged her body back inside. I cut the rope, unraveled the back table covers, and out rolled a grotesque Jen. She rolled several feet before stopping near the upside-down couch. Her left leg was in an unnatural position, high above her head, but I didn't care. It was nice knowing you, Jen Walker. I went outside and took a branch that had some leaves from the ground, and shook the loose dirt to cover my tracks. I texted the number to let them know I had the grafts, then I lifted the heavy cooler, and forced myself to march to my car. Every several yards I had to stop and rest. I finally managed to get to my car. Of course, dear readers, you would expect me to have a house far removed from everyone's without street lights, and you'd be right. I unlocked my car door, put the box inside. By that time, I received a text telling me where to place the box. That was that.

You don't know how wiped out I am relating this story to you, folks. But one thing I did glean from my experience with Jen Walker, I had to find out if she did really have an uncle in the police force, and if she had told him about her suspicions.

April 7th

I went online and found some articles on Detective Jay Club. He was a nine-year veteran who had solved numerous unsolved mysteries. Well, la de da for him. His record was spotless; his partner was Detective Ralph Peterson, blah, blah, blah. There was nothing that would indicate a niece, or a family member. I read, again, about his wife and daughter both dying in childbirth. Maybe I was a little callous to him on the phone when I told him about the prostitute, but screw it. His wife and daughter had died when he first entered the police department nine years ago. Get over it, Jay! Trying living with something that can't be removed and you're mercilessly beaten and made fun of all the time. That is, unless you're a zillionaire. Then a dermatologist could probably fix it. And who the hell knew what I would look like after the surgery? It could be worse. After a little more searching, I came across a picture of Detective Jay Club with a woman. It was a recent picture, probably of him and his girlfriend. She was beautiful. She was way too good for him. The print was small under their picture; I barely managed to read her name. Brittany Schott. Did I say she was beautiful? Hmm, I may have to pay attention to this woman. Who knows, she may end up being another one of my victims. It would be a shame to cut open someone like that, but money was money.

Then I looked up Jen Walker on various social platforms, looked at her friends and family. To my utter amazement, she wasn't kidding. Detective Jay Club was her uncle. She never told me who was her uncle, but now I knew. It did change things. When Jay found out his niece had been killed by the same M.O. as the other poor saps, he'll go ballistic and go on a manhunt. It's now become personal. That wasn't my intention, but I had to do something after she suspected me. Dear readers, you know what would be funny? If one of Jay's friends, or he himself, needed a bone or skin donation, and his niece was where the graft came from. Highly unlikely since she wasn't tested, and I didn't find out anything about her medical history, but still, it could be construed as funny, right?

April 11th

By now, perceptive readers, a question may come to your minds. In my entries, I have killed three people but I haven't stated much about the police, being questioned, or anything germane to the killing spree. Fear not, because as of yet, they have no clues. The police did find Jen's rotten, stench-ridden body because the smell permeated the area, and one of the teenage kids that frequented the shack with his girlfriend, found her. Detective Jay Club swore he would catch the serial killer. The label serial killer didn't strike my fancy because, while I was killing them for pleasure, trust me on that one, but I was doing it for profit too. And on the other side of that coin, the recipients of said body parts, who I procured, will have their lives enhanced. (Except if my father, the prostitute, or Jen harbored some disease I didn't know about). Nothing to fear, dear readers, I made sure no fingerprints, or any other traceable evidence would be there. I found the police went to people's houses to ask questions about Jen Walker, but they never went to my neck of the woods.

April 15th

Huh, go figure. The police came to my door today. They went to my mother's house, and she actually had my address. Didn't think she really cared. It was then I realized, of course she cared. How else would she get her cigarettes, alcohol, and food?

The Detectives weren't Jay Club or Ralph Peterson. It was two Detectives I never saw before. They were sympathetic when they told me about my father's passing. I displayed the right amount of caring, but firm enough to let them know, he'd been out of my life since my birth. I didn't get into any of the details. Then they probed.

The smaller cop asked, "We also have two other murders besides your father. One was a prostitute, and the other a nurse named Jen Walker who worked in Indianapolis. Did you know any of them?"

Friends, if they didn't already know I knew Jen, they would with the mall cameras, or people that saw Jen and me publicly disagreeing. I couldn't lie about that one. "I've never been with a prostitute, and don't intend to, but I briefly met Jen at the mall in the food court."

Larger cop, "Did you guys talk?"

"Yes, the food court was full, and I was alone at

the outermost table. She asked if she could sit down. I said yes."

Smaller cop, "That's it?"

"No, we discussed how society viewed my birthmark because I was wearing a hoodie and sunglasses. She thought I should not wear anything to hide my true self. Yes, she used true self several times."

Larger cop, "Is that all?"

"We had a different take on society's perspective. She had never been in my shoes. In the end we agreed to disagree."

Small cop, "Did you leave with her?"

Large cop, small cop. I started to wonder if they were using bad cop, good cop on me. But I remained calm. "Yes and no."

Large cop, "I don't understand. Did you leave with Jen Walker or not?"

"Yes, we left the food court together. We found that we parked close by in the parking lot. Her car was parked up front; mine a little more in the back so I had to pass her car first."

Small cop, "So, you didn't make plans to go out again, or exchange phone numbers?"

"Officer, look at me. I have never, ever been on a date in my life. We most certainly did not exchange phone numbers."

Large cop, "Can I see your phone?"

See readers, that's why I told Jen I didn't want her number. It could come back and haunt me. "Of course." I handed him my cell that was on the coffee table in front of us. The large cop took a pair of reading glasses from his front pocket, put them on, and started fidgeting with my phone. I was racking my brain to see whose numbers I had. After I started to freelance tissue procurement, I took the name of the tissue company I work for out of my contacts just to be safe, and just inserted their number.

While the large cop looked at my phone, the smaller cop said, "Your mom said you buy her cigarettes, and food. We saw a lot of alcohol. Do you drive her around?"

I smiled. "No. She doesn't like to leave the house. I am her taxi service. She calls me, tells me what she wants, then I get it for her."

"How often is that?"

"About twice a week."

"She said you worked as a receiving clerk at some pantry store. She couldn't remember the name of it."

"My mother's memory isn't what it used to be. I haven't worked there in years. The employees and bosses there have a high turnover rate."

"So, where do you work now?"

"At a company that makes tissues." Wasn't lying, but I was betting they were like most non-medical people who thought tissue was something you used to blow your nose.

The large cop finished what he was doing. He looked to the smaller cop, and nodded.

Large cop, "Thank you. Here's my card should you think of anything that could help us in the investigation."

"No problem, thank you." See folks, nothing to worry about. They walked to their vehicle, and left without another word. Within five minutes of the Detectives leaving, my cell rang telling me I had an hour to be at the tissue company. I had a procurement to go to. I wondered what body parts I would be taking out this time!

April 18th

Remember the gun I took before I killed Jen? I had some free time so I drove to the hospital Jen told me she worked at. I presumed nurses worked twelve hour shifts because that's what they did on drama TV shows. I had done some procurement's at hospitals but I never thought to ask nurses how many hours their shift was. I imagined they probably started their morning shift at seven. I got to the hospital around seven in the evening, and drove around the parking lot. But dear readers, that parking lot was huge! How the hell was I going to find AJ's car? I knew what he looked like because of social media, but the picture of him was blurry. I rolled down my window when I saw several people walk to their respective cars. I paid special attention to keep my right side of my face in full view, and pretend I was looking for a parking spot. I managed to overhear a conversation between two guys. "Hey Michael, did you see what AJ bought for lunch? He bought about two pounds of nachos!"

"God, I couldn't even eat a half a pound of that stuff." The guy Michael turned around. "Hey AJ, how can you eat that stuff?"

I found a parking spot when my ears perked up. I looked behind the two guys. I saw a stocky guy with a full red beard walk confidently toward them. Yup, that was him! The two guys slowed down, and the three of them walked together. AJ stopped at his car, remotely unlocked it, and put his hand on the side of his door. "I could probably eat four pounds of that stuff! It was good!" AJ laughed for a few seconds until he heard something. He checked his pockets. He withdrew a phone that was ringing. "Hello? Yeah, I forgot to put back the phone. Can I just give it to you tomorrow?" His bearded face creased, and then he sighed heavily. "Okay, okay, I'll return it!" He hung up, and looked at his two friends. "I forgot the damned phone, and they need it for the next shift. I have to go back to surgery. See you guys tomorrow."

AJ started walking back to the hospital. I didn't know where surgery was located inside, but I figured after the crowd thinned, I would have ample time to hatch my scheme. Quickly, I ransacked my medical bag looking for something I knew I had. Ah, found it! Packing tape. I had to tape the box of body parts closed before I brought it to the location pickup. When no one else came out, and the parking lot was empty, I took the gun that was in the bag that had Jen's prints on it, put it in my jacket pocket, took a piece of packing tape, walked to AJ's car, and remembered where AJ had touched his car door, and put the tape over it, pressed against it, and took it off. I saw his fingerprints! I looked around and darkness was falling. The lights in the parking lot weren't on yet, so it was a perfect time to take the gun out (with gloves on, dear readers), then attached the tape that had AJ's fingerprints on it, to the gun. Then I took the tape off, and remembered AJ had not re-locked his car door. I would have heard it. Looking all around, I quickly took the gun, and placed it underneath his front seat. I practically ran to my car, and headed home. I was going to use the voice changer I had bought, and make an anonymous phone call.

April 22nd

Folks, my plan didn't go as I expected. In the paper, the police said they brought AJ Mandary in for questioning. They had found his fingerprints on Jen's gun. Had I thought this through, I should have taken more prints and put them all over the shack. That would have placed him at the scene of the crime, and then there would have been more concrete evidence. I didn't bother to read if he was released or not. I presumed he would have. So, AJ Mandry, I have decided you're going to be my red herring. I now know what you look like, and what car you drive.

April 27th

Dear readers, finding the next candidate was a piece of cake. Actually, more like Chinese food. I was at a Chinese restaurant. Since the police knew I had been at the mall, why give them any more visibility when I could go to a regular business with no cameras. I was waiting in line when I noticed a tall African American gentleman standing in front of me. He had to be six-foot six inches tall, and was on the thin side, maybe one hundred ninety, two hundred pounds, and bald. He was looking at the menu while I was scanning him. He had pants on, so I couldn't tell how good his skin was... for now. He seemed to be in his late twenties, so that was a definite plus because it meant I could conceivably take a lot of his parts. However, I noticed the grafts my client wanted started to change. I had to text them explaining who the person was, and what they looked like. I never had to do that before. They started the new process with the email after I dropped off Jen's body parts in the cooler. I was assuming based on my assessment of my target, they would tell me what body parts they wanted. Odd, but hey, the money was good.

Now readers, when I tell you I was getting excited to the point of getting nervous, sweating like bullets, and having to pee, please don't deduce I wanted him in a sexual manner. No, I wanted to do surgery on the bastard. He might be a good man, a family man, or he might be a smoker and drinker. *I did not care.* I lost caring about the human race the day I was old enough to recognize I was shunned by the discoloration of my entire left side of my body. So dammit, if I wanted to kill this tall person with his Tall Legs... then it hit me, dear readers. Right there and then, until I killed him, his nickname was going to be Tall Legs. Now reader, I know what you're thinking. Why name someone you're going to possibly de-skin and de-bone? Because it made watching Tall Legs all the more exciting! What I wanted was going to be mine! He simply had no choice. I watched Tall Legs finish ordering his Chinese food and wait nearby. He glanced my way while I pretended to read the menu because I already knew what I wanted. I ordered shrimp with lobster sauce, and a large won-tong soup. I could tell he was looking at the left side of my face before leaving. I had another hoodie on. This one didn't cover up nearly the amount of my face as the other hoodie I usually wore but sometimes ya gotta wash your clothes. Since I had to wash my clothes at my mother's house, I didn't wash them too often. There were times I found her moldy clothes were left in the washer because she had forgotten about them. I had to run the washer machine empty with a lot of bleach before I would wash my clothes in that washer.

I came out of my daydream. I tend to do that,

dear readers. Now I was angry. He had stared at my face! How dare he look at my face when I was going to kill him? Didn't he know how I longed for this, that this was my *sole purpose* in life? Oh, Tall Legs, I thought, I can't wait until I get my surgical hands on you! We both waited in silence. Both of our food was ready nearly at the same time. With two cashiers, we ended up leaving at the same time. My quarry walked fast with those long legs. I barely managed to keep him in my sight. Once outside, the sun glared. Folks, when I tell you it was bright, I thought my retinas were singed. As luck would have it, I had parked only two rows over from Tall Legs. It was destiny. It was as if God himself said, "Ben, he's all yours, take what you want!" Soon Tall Legs and I pulled out of the parking lot, and went east on 96th street heading toward Castleton. Tall Legs went north on Cumberland road and entered Fishers. He turned right on 116th street and made a right on Hoosier road, not far from a golf course.

Tall Legs pulled into a driveway and I memorized the number. I continued on, pretending I had a destination to go to while checking out the scenery. There weren't too many trees near the golf course but Tall Leg's house had ample foliage and trees. I nonchalantly turned around at the end of the road and passed the house again. I saw him meet his wife on the stoops near the front door and give her a kiss. Great, now I not only had to figure out Tall Leg's schedule but his wife's as well. But, that shouldn't be a problem. I had two days before my client wanted their product.

I returned home happy. I had a next victim, and I had not been caught. Nothing but smooth sailing from here, folks!

April 28th

At five the next morning I woke up. I had set the alarm so I could tail Tall Legs. I drove with anticipation as I played the scene out in my mind of what I was going to do with my next victim. It was a thrilling experience I enjoyed before every person I abducted. Satisfied, I realized I was close to Tall Legs road. I parked in the parking lot of a strip mall near Tall Leg's road, and made sure there weren't any cameras. I would be able to tail him once his car passed by. I didn't have to wait long. Allowing three car lengths distance, I found out where he worked. It was at a financial center not far from his house on 96th street. So Tall Legs was a financial planner? I would seek out some advice before the psychological and physical torture began.

Now all I had to do was to see where his wife worked. Rushing back to Hoosier road, I managed to see a car pull out of his driveway. I nonchalantly turned around, pretended I was lost, went back to the strip mall, and waited for Tall Leg's wife to pass.

She passed a minute later and I followed her at a discreet distance. Tall Leg's wife was a speed demon! She ran through all of the yellow lights and drove like a manic. I didn't want to get pulled over so I avoided her pitfalls but still managed to track her to Keystone at the Crossing, not too far from the fashion mall on

86th street. I waited for her to get out of the car and walk several yards before I left my car. She walked into one of the tall buildings and got into the elevator as I walked through the front entrance. I wasn't worried. All I had to do was see which floor the elevator stopped on. It was the tenth floor. I found a legend and looked at all the businesses on the tenth floor. I realized there were too many to single out which business she worked at, I made a rash decision. I decided to forgo the woman, and derail her from reaching her house after work this evening. That would give me plenty of time to grab Tall Legs before his wife got home. I left the building and found her vehicle. I went to my car, extracted a sharp knife, and walked slowly over to Tall Legs wife's car. With utter care I looked around to make sure no one was looking, and no cameras were around, I took the knife and flatten all four of her tires. The seepage of air from the tires was music to my ears as the seepage of blood was music to my eyes. By the time they figured out it was sabotage, it would be too late for her husband. I pulled out of the parking lot more confident than ever.

I got called in to work and could barely concentrate. I didn't have to go on a recovery, I had to read more updated S.O.P.'s, and sign that I had read them. It would take all day! But people asked me stupid questions and I tried to act normal. Didn't they realize on the day of my plans of killing someone, I wanted to be left alone? I had to work today and then abduct Tall Legs at his house this evening. When four thirty rolled around, folks, I'll tell you, I practically ran out the door. I tried not to rush to his house. I had decided to park at the parking lot of the strip mall near his home. When I got out, I tried to alter my walk as I strolled down Hoosier road. It was getting dark, which was a plus on my side. Out of my peripheral vision, I didn't detect anyone staring at me.

When I got to the house I found a place in the front where the bushes on both sides of the stairs leading to Tall Legs house would be a perfect cover. I had my medical bag close to me, along with the box which I barely was able to sandwich underneath my long jacket, made me screech inwardly with delight. I checked my watch. It wouldn't be long.

Twenty minutes later, Tall Legs pulled into his driveway. It was already dark as the garage door opened and his car leisurely rolled inside. I ducked behind his car, ran into the garage, and staked myself on the other side of the idling car. Quietly and quickly, I extracted the cattle prod while the guy was busy on the phone, and closed the garage door. I had bought a cattle prod with cash at a store that sold tractors, and other items for farms while on a procurement far from my home. The other techs were still eating when I noticed the store across the street. If I was going to have fun with my victims, I would need to stop using ether. I wanted them awake. I heard Tall Legs on the phone.

"Okay, honey, just call Triple A and let them tow the car. I don't know how you got four tires flat but I know it will cost a lot of money! Alright honey, just do it. I know you'll be home late, it's okay. I will make something quick and easy for me. When you get your car fixed, you can stop somewhere to eat. Yeah I know, what happened to the tightwad husband! Yeah, it's alright, eat and come home. Okay honey. Bye, love you!"

Tall Legs hung up and opened the door in the garage that led inside. I quickly ran too. I didn't want to be stuck inside the garage all night. Luckily, I had picked up on the conversation. So, the wife would have the car towed, get the car fixed and find somewhere to eat, good it would provide more time for me to get acquainted with Tall Legs! Tall Legs went inside and walked into his kitchen. He walked to the refrigerator, opened it and peered inside without even looking behind him. He reached in and grabbed the container and opened it. I smelled meatloaf. When he turned around he came face to face with me.

Before he had a chance to speak or react, I lunged at him with the cattle prod. Instantly, the container of food fell to the floor and spilled all over the linoleum floor. Tall Legs went down to the ground. I kept hitting him with the prod until he didn't move. I reached down to my medical bag, took out rope, and tied him up. I dragged him to the living room. When he became coherent, he was looking up at me, his abductor.

"Hi Tall Legs, how are you?" I thought I would start out polite before I sought out financial advice.

"Who the hell are you and what are you doing in my house?" The tall man's voice was cold and hard.

"First question is unimportant. You don't need to know who I am. The second question is self-explanatory. Actually, I am wrong. You are going to help a lot of people with your body parts..."

Tall Legs eyes went wide. "What the fuck are you talking about? No way am I going to allow you to take anything from me!"

I put a gloved finger to his lips. "You'll need to be quiet or I'm afraid I'm going to have to hurt you."

"You're going to hurt me regardless so why shouldn't I yell? Help! Help!!"

"Well, there you go! Good point Tall Legs." I bent down and punched him in the jaw. Instantly the man's face swelled. "What's your name, Tall Legs?"

"Fuck off."

"That's no way to speak to a stranger in your home about to kill you!" Really, Tall Legs? All I wanted was his name. See the shit I have to put up with, dear readers?

"Oh really? Try this; fuck you!"

He was being really disrespectful. What happened to manners these days? I hit him on the jaw, in his eyes, and his ears. I waited a second to catch my breath. "Tell me your name, now!"

"Okay, okay! Andre. Andre King."

"Sounds like a made up name to me. I'll ask one more time. What's your name?"

"You can look in my wallet! I am Andre King!"

I bent down, and smacked him across his face. "Don't yell, Andre Tall Legs King." I looked around his small house, and found the nearest bedroom. "I am going to drag you to your room. Under no circumstances will you make any noise, is that clear Andre King Tall Legs?"

He was about to open his mouth when I took out the cattle prod and struck him in his throat. His eyes went behind his sockets. Dragging him proved difficult. Finally, I managed to place him in his room. He had a television on the wall. I found the remote, and turned it on. I put up the volume loud because the dermatome will make a lot of noise. See dear readers, always thinking! Now that Andre was positioned the way I wanted him, I had to ask him some questions. "Andre, besides surgically removing your body parts, a rather painful process for you, I am in your house to ask some financial questions. That is the only reason why I haven't taped your mouth shut." I sat down beside him and started rubbing his legs with my gloved hand. Andre squirmed, and cringed away. "Now, Andre, calm down. I have some questions. I'm expecting some good money with your body parts, and I wanted to know where to invest. Should I go mutual funds, start an IRA or the stock market? Or is there something you would recommend that I don't know about? What's your advice?"

The man on the bed seemed to me that he couldn't believe what he was hearing. He was probably thinking was the psycho really serious? As if I was reading his mind, I answered for him. "Andre, I need a quick answer about my financial needs. I was thinking the IRA was my best bet in the long run. But the stock market is a long-term investment strategy too since I am still pretty young. And I would have to consider the commission involved too. See my quandary? So which strategy would you recommend?" I saw the confusion in his eyes, then something akin to a plan. "I know what you're thinking; I see it in your eyes. You're thinking if I stall this person long enough, my wife would be home, and able to call the police. I know your wife won't be home for a long time. By the way, you even let her buy dinner before she came home. That's very generous of you. And I will let you in on a little secret between the two of us now that we're friends. I am the one who gave her the four flat tires." I figured honesty was the best policy.

Andre's eyes lit up in terror. He started to whimper. Typical, I thought. When they faced their mortality, and knew with certainty they couldn't do anything, crying was the first response. But I was a compassionate man, wasn't I readers? I stroked his bald head and whispered to him, "How fortunate you were in being chosen! Just think how much your body parts would benefit others!" But Andre still cried. "Well, well. The strong silent type, huh? Let's get started since you aren't going to give me any financial advice I was seeking. Damn, I was really hoping you would've helped me, Andre. But since you won't, and are being childish about dispensing financial advice, I'll have to put socks in your mouth. I think I'll use the ones you wore all day."

Andre King struggled, and started to yell. I bent down and repeatedly punched him in the mouth, face, and nose and for good measure; I punched him in the stomach. The beating finally took the fire out of him.

I laughed. "It's going to be okay, Andre." I took out my bag of surgical supplies and put all of the sterile items onto the sterile field I had made. I had to put two back table covers under Andre's body because he was so long. I scrubbed my hands in his kitchen sink, put on my sterile attire, and draped both sides of his legs using a sterile drape. They had a peel off so I could adhere the sterile drape to each side of his lower extremities. I failed you readers as I didn't drape the sides of the other victims for better sterility. My bad. Oh well. Then I started cleaning the man's posterior back and his posterior legs.

I could tell Andre was frozen in fear. But I didn't care. I continued with the procedure. I didn't want to go too fast because I didn't want to nick the grafts or I wouldn't be paid. The client was adamant about that too. After the mineral oil was spread on him, I took the dermatome and clicked it on. I realized the noise was loud and turned it off. I walked around the small abode until I found a radio and turned it on full blast. It should mask the noise. "Now, my good friend, Andre King, I will share something with you. I have taken skin from African American males and females. Did you know that after taking their skin at eighteenth of one inch, it is white? I only say this because I was thinking of using the dermatome on the left side of my body, minus my face, of course, and see if the skin that remained would be the color of my other side. What do you think?" Andre mumbled incoherently but then again, he did have his two dirty socks in his mouth, and I wasn't going to remove them. I got to work. Occasionally I would stop the machine and look at his face and try to gauge when he would pass out from the pain. Or I would slap him in the face to wake him up. I smiled. I was having fun and getting paid at the same time!

After I was done removing Andre's skin, I saw with satisfaction, that he was still alive. His chest was going up and down. Dear readers, you don't know the exhilaration I was feeling right now! I wanted to share the good news with Andre King. "Guess what, Andre? I am not going to take any of your tendons. No, the client was specific. Skin was always needed for burn victims. And I'm not taking all of your bones, but I am going to take your saphenous veins, and what is called a knee block from you. I see by your face, with your eyes barely opened, that you don't understand. Let me shed some light on you. You probably know what your saphenous veins are. They run down the length of your leg from where the femoral artery is all the way down to your toes. But for your knee block, I will take my four fingers, and place them right above your kneecap. That will be the proximal, or the top portion of the knee block. And the bottom or distal portion is right about here." I moved my hand down past his kneecap, and placed it about half way down his fibula. "But Andre, I must first cut out your saphenous veins!"

I had to find them first. It usually lay on the respective side of the ankle bone and I found it with ease. I carefully cut the uppermost top of the skin using a sterile scalpel, located the vein, cut underneath the vein so just a section of the vein protruded. I had to infuse the vein using a 60mm syringe filled with RPI fluid to make sure there were no clots. It was called flushing.

After waiting the required fifteen minutes, I took a pair of mayo's (clamps), and using another sterile scalpel, cut along the path of the saphenous, being careful to cut close to the uppermost portion of the skin. I looked at Andre. He was motionless. "Andre, wake the fuck up!" Nothing. I figured he was in too much pain to respond so I resumed.

Sometimes the vein lay just below the surface, and if you went too deep you would cut the vein in two. I have done that a few times early in my career. It happens. I traced the vein behind the knee, and went back up toward the femoral artery. It was a painstakingly slow procedure because I wanted to be careful and not cut it. When I was done, there was an open incision from four inches above the hip bone to down below the Achilles tendon (heel). I went to the upper part of the leg, and found where the saphenous vein met the femoral artery. I peeled the skin, cut the top portion of the muscle and pulled it down. The femoral artery lay underneath. I needed to clamp the femoral to make sure no blood would be come out before taking the saphenous vein out. I am a stickler for details, folks. Don't want too much blood on me because sometimes the wetness can cause slipperiness, and I didn't want the blade to slip from my grasp and cut me.

Cautiously, I peeled the skin back from both sides using a sterile scalpel blade. I was careful not to cut the tributaries, which were where the saphenous veins branched off. I needed those to come out too. Sometimes the tributaries were shaped like the number eight when they came along with the saphenous.

Finally, I used a pair of sterile mayo's (clamps), and slowly cut under the vein and on both sides until the vein was in my hands. The right side was out. Now I had to do the same thing for the left side. I put the two veins in separate containers and marked on each one which side they came from. I placed them in two sterile bags.

"Andre, I'm pretty sure you're dead but I'm going to talk to you anyway. Now, you might ask yourself a question. How is this skilled procurement specialist going to take my knee block like I told you about earlier? Great question!" I patted him on his dead head. "You didn't stay with me, Andre. I didn't want you to die until at least I explained more of the surgical process. Dying on me was rude on your part!" Here I am trying to educate the man on a surgical procedure, and he croaked on me! Some people! I took the scalpel blade from the sterile field and made the usual initial incision just above his hip bone. When the scalpel moved slowly down his left leg, down the side of his skin, I was the one who moaned, but in ecstasy! I didn't have to worry about the fascia or the tendons, so I was able to cut down to the bone, specifically the thigh bone, and the fibula. I was going to leave the muscle attached to the kneecap so the bone was still attached to the knee block. I went around the kneecap, avoiding it. Instead of going all the way down to his toes, I stopped just to the point where the Tibula was attached to the Fibula (The two bones that go from the kneecap to the foot). I replaced a pair of sterile gloves, my blade, and cut Andre's skin on both sides of his left leg that it exposed his tissue (muscle) and his bones. I felt around on one side of his thighbone, and cut the muscle that surrounded it. I did the same to his other side, and the top and bottom too. I looked to Andre. Sorry Andre, I'm sure you were a nice man, but I had to do this. I will not go to your funeral because

117

oftentimes the murder returns to the scene of the crime, or sees what the victim's family sees. I enjoy doing this too much to be caught.

I repeated the process of removing his flesh from his Fibula. Then I took a Gigli saw wire (while there are a few types of wires, I used a thin wire that had tiny razor edges on both sides) that had a small circle at the end of each wire so a handle could be inserted through it. Then using my four fingers like before, went just above his kneecap, mentally marked where it was, and took the Gigli blade, placed it on the top of the femur bone where I had mentally marked it, and started going back and forth like you would with a saw when you cut wood. I applied more pressure as the razor caught hold of the bone. I went back and forth until I went through the thigh bone. The smell of burnt flesh and bone was an aroma that turned me on! I went down to his Fibula, and found the spot I wanted, and put the Gigli saw on top of the bone, and went back and forth until it cut clean through both the Fibula, and the Tibula. I took the knee block, and scrambled to find the long clear bags I always used when removing bones. I finally found them, and placed the knee block into the clear bag that was marked, took off a pair of gloves, and put a fresh pair on. Next I had to do the other side.

After I was done cleaning Andre's house where no evidence would indict me, and had Andre's body parts in the cooler (the ice would be bought before I went to the secret location this time).

Dear readers, I want you to know how much of a pleasurable experience it was, especially as I am relating the details to you via the voice software on my laptop. But it's close to midnight, and Mr. Orderly will be making his rounds soon. How I loathed that man! I daresay I don't think there is anyone more with more malevolence than him.

May 4th

Mr. Orderly had come by today. It was my birthday, and he brought a chocolate cup cake for me. I thought to myself that perhaps for the first time he would be nice to me. That thought lasted five seconds. He brought the cupcake to me with a single candle. It would be hard pressed for me to use my hands to eat it. I could, mind you, but it would be difficult. He came to my bed where I was sitting upright against my pillow. He told me to blow out the candle. When I leaned in to blow it out, he moved the cupcake away. He told me to blow the candle out again. I did that three times before I told him to piss off; I didn't want his damned cupcake. Apparently, that was the wrong thing to say to him. He removed the candle, and put the candle close to my face. I backed as far away as possible. Mr. Orderly continued to taunt me until his amusement wore off. He put the cupcake on the table, took the candle, and without warning, took my right arm, held it up, and thrust the candle in my armpit until the candle went out. With his other hand, he held my mouth until my screaming subsided into whimpering. "Happy birthday, freak!" He said. He took the cupcake, and forced it into my mouth, laughed, then walked out whistling.

Dear readers, I never really believed in Karma until that incident. That event, and all the other dastardly deeds he has inflicted upon me culminated in that eye awakening revelation. I need some alone time to heal the physical and emotional damage I just went through.

May 15th

I had received an email which stated my client only wanted the skin, and the heart. I was disappointed until I realized I could give my client those grafts, but that didn't mean I couldn't torture my next victim. I had contemplated who my next victim would be. On social media, AJ was friends with another nurse named Jenni Nazimek.

Jenni worked at a different hospital than AJ, but, according to their online social status, they frequented the same bars. I even knew what Jenni looked like. Gotta love the internet. And, to my utter amazement, both were headed to a bar in Castleton, Indiana. In fact, a group of people were getting together to celebrate a nurse's retirement tomorrow night. As luck would have it, I wasn't on call tomorrow so I was free to contemplate a plan, and think about contingencies in case something went wrong.

I was practically salivating the next day, dear readers. I was eager to procure Jenni's skin and heart. I waited at the far end of the parking lot. It was starting to get dark later here in Indiana. Because of that I had to wait until later in the night to get here. The bar was in a strip mall adjacent to the main mall, and cars overflowed from there, into the parking lot I was parked in. That made finding my next victim difficult. Not impossible, but just a little harder.

At one point, I had fallen asleep in my car, and awoke in a panic. Did I miss her? I checked my phone. It was just after eleven pm. I noticed a great deal of cars were gone because the mall had been closed for the last couple of hours. Damn! I waited another half an hour but I was getting antsy. I was about to start my car, leave in utter disappointment, and disgusted with myself when a few people exited the bar. I took my high-powered binoculars, and scanned the people. There were three women, and one of them was Jenni! They were laughing, and giggling hysterically about something. I couldn't hear them, but I didn't care what trivial discourse escaped their lips. I was focused on one thing and one thing only. My quarry. The three ladies chatted for a long time. Jesus, Jenni, stop the fucking talking, get in your car, and let me kill you! Was I asking too much? Finally, they said their goodbyes. I started my car and followed Jenni from a distance. Me thinks Jenni drank a little too much. She was veering from left to right. Three scenarios entered my mind immediately. One is she would be pulled over by the police, and that would set me back a few days. Two is she would get into a car accident, and possibly become a donor without my intervention. Or three, nothing would occur and I could de-skin her and de-heart her tonight as planned.

After several more minutes of following her at a discreet distance, I heard sirens in the background, and saw flashing lights. At first I thought it was an ambulance, or a fire truck. But soon I saw it was a police car so I slowed my speed, pretended to play with the radio as the cop car flew past me, and pulled Jenni over. Damn, that's the last thing I wanted to happen! I slowly passed the police and Jenni. The cop was questioning her. As I passed them, I realized I had two options. I could either hope to find out on social media, or the local paper had a page that told of DUI's, assaults, etc., if she was arrested (because dear readers, she was driving erratically), when she would be released, or find another victim. I chose the former rather than the latter. Once I have a victim in my brain, it's hard to change my mind.

Dear readers, Jenni spent the entire weekend in jail. She had mentioned her incarceration briefly on social media. But the brevity told me much. She was out, and free. I didn't care when her hearing was, or what ramifications transpired. I only wanted her. Trouble was, my client emailed and asked me what the delay was. I emailed them back, and told them I had been called into work a lot lately. I was procuring about two to three cases a day. If they would be patient, I would get them their skin and heart. And to make matters worse my mother called me when I was about to get on the internet and see what Jenni had planned for this coming weekend. That's what was so great about social media. People posted their plans so criminals, and people like me who wanted to procure their body parts, knew when they wouldn't be home, and where they would be.

I reluctantly called my mother back after she called me several more times. I did all I could to take out the loathing I felt for her when I spoke with her. She wanted some alcohol, and she wanted it right there and then. I told her no, but she was insistent. I told her okay, but decided I had more important things to do. Hopefully, the bitch passes out watching senseless TV shows. My more immediate concern was with Jenni. I went to her homepage. She was going to the same bar Friday night. Okay, two more days. They should go fast.

May 21st

Folks, the two days ended up going slow. I worked around the clock for one and a half of those days. If we had procurement more than a hundred miles away, we had to pack for two cases. The team drove the company van to Evansville, then we found out we had to drive to Madison, the other side of the state for another case. I fell into my bed with my clothes on. I was thankful I did not put myself on call tonight, and the weekend. I checked my cell, and my mother had called fifteen times. Oh, sorry mother. I forgot about your fucking alcohol needs, and not my money needs, so I can have money for your alcohol needs.

I checked my cell again. It was eight in the morning; I could sleep well into the afternoon, get my mother her alcohol, and go to the bar. Jenni never made it to her house that night, so I couldn't surprise her there; I had to go to the bar to track her back to her house. Man Jenni, you're making my life difficult, you know that? All I wanted to do is remove some of your body parts! Geez, will ya at least help me with that small request?

I woke up at four in the afternoon, took a much needed shower, nuked some left over spam, slapped it on some toast, and then thought about my itinerary tonight. One thing I forgot about was I had to go back to the hospital where AJ worked, and get more fingerprints from his car. That put a damper on things. God, all I wanted to do was procure some body parts, which was easy for me, but when you add all the bullshit I had to do to make that happen, you'd realize what a difficult process it was, dear readers. Can't you see why I got so frustrated all of the time?

I pulled into the liquor store's parking lot, and noticed they had installed a camera. Did every place have a freaking camera? Technology was a great tool to stalk someone, but sucked when they tracked you. To make matters worse, there was a new cashier, and not the usual guy I knew, Tony. So, I am more than sure he thought it suspect when I entered the store in a hoodie and sunglasses. I nonchalantly asked him where Tony was to try to make him more placid. He probably had a gun behind the counter. Thankfully nothing was said, and I bought alcohol without incident, except for the fact I had to show ID. Tony knew I was a regular so he never asked for ID even though you're supposed to. Here's another thing I thought about when I put the bags of alcohol in the front seat of the passenger side. How much alcohol do I buy my mother? If I bought only a bottle or two, she would call me a few days later demanding more. If I bought her several bottles, like I did today, she would drink more because she had more, and call me in four or five days. I can't win with that woman.

Anyway, that was my problem, dear readers, not yours. I left her house screaming at her, but the anguish I felt dissipated once I left my former abode, and drove to the hospital. I now knew AJ's car, and found he parked it almost in the same spot, which told me he liked routine, or he was lazy and didn't want to walk any further than he had to. I couldn't find a spot, and didn't want to park in front of his car and draw suspicion, so I opted to find the closest spot, which was two rows over. I casually walked to his car, pretending I was walking toward the hospital entrance. Quickly I took a long piece of clear packing tape so I wouldn't have to do this every time I wanted to kill someone AJ knew, and methodically placed the long strip just above the car door handle. I pulled it away, and found several fingerprints. I would cut them into strips when I had the time, probably after the recovery was finished. I refused to look around to see if anyone saw me because I didn't want to draw attention to myself. That being done, I went through the drive through at McDonalds, ordered twenty-piece nugget with sweet and sour sauce with a doctor pepper. I had a couple of hours to kill, pun intended.

I drove to the bar and parked where I had parked the last time. So maybe I liked routine too. I dozed off, and awoke when it was dark. Last time she came out late, and was very drunk. This time would Jenni not drink too much, come to her car early, or would she drink in excess like last time? These are the things I had to think about, people.

It was a quarter to eleven when she came out of the door. She left alone, and walked straight to her car. When she got in, she punched the steering wheel, yelled some incomprehensible nonsense, started her car, stayed there for another few seconds, punched the steering wheel again, then put her foot to the metal, and high tailed out of there. I was caught off guard, started my car, and managed to locate her about a half a mile down the road. Before I killed her tonight, I would have to ask her what was wrong. I like to know people's idiosyncrasies.

Thankfully, she seemed sober. She drove from 82nd street east all the way to where it met Fall Creek road. She made a right and drove a couple of blocks, and made a right. I had to be careful and survey my surroundings. It was an older community based on the trees in the neighborhood. The trees were more mature, so I knew the houses had been there awhile. She pulled into a small yellow ranch house halfway down the block. I passed her house to see if she would open the garage door, and I would be screwed because I wouldn't have time to park the car, get out, retrieve my medical bag, run, and dodge my presence before the door came all the way down. My concern was unfounded as I parked nearby where there wasn't a lamp post. She stayed in the car, and seemed to be talking to someone on her phone. The conversation turned heated as she got out of her car. I was able to walk behind her without notice, which really surprised me. She barely managed to hold the phone to her ear, and unlock her front door. I quickly stepped inside as she slammed the door closed without turning around. She was still on her phone. Score another plus for technology. Distraction. There was a closet door that was slightly ajar. I hid all the way to the right side of the closet. Jenni's footsteps became more pronounced as she came closer to the closet where I was hiding. Evidently, she got off the phone since I didn't hear any conversation. I heard her lock the front door, and come toward the closet. Right, she was going to hang her jacket. Perfect. I heard her clothes rustle as she took her jacket off. She was about to grasp a plastic hanger when I lunged out, and punched her in the face. Her eyes went wide with disbelief, and she opened her mouth before she fell to the ground. I didn't give her a chance to recuperate as blow after blow came down to her pretty face. It was time to get to work. I noticed Jenni had turned on the outside light after she had locked the front door. I couldn't have that when I was completed and had to leave. I turned it off, went back to Jenni's inert body. I slapped her until she became awake. You should have seen her face when she looked around, found she was immobile, her TV was on, and the curtains were drawn; only the dimmest of light was on. Before I started on her skin, I promised myself I wanted to know why she was so upset. I slapped her one more time so she would focus on me. "I have a question for you, pretty lady. I was concerned when you came out of the bar tonight, you seemed upset, and banged on the steering wheel. What gives?"

"Were you following me?"

"Of course, I was. I followed you the night you got pulled over too. Let me tell ya something sweetheart, you were drunk!"

"Why were you following me?"

"I will tell you why only if you tell me why you were so upset."

"Why do you give a shit?"

I sat down beside her, just outside the sterile field I had created. "Because I care about people."

"If you cared about people, I wouldn't be tied up, on the floor, and nude."

"Touché. Boy, aren't you the smart nurse. But really I do care because, believe it or not, I am a humanist. I am all for the enhancement of people's lives. Case in point is me. Look at my skin discoloration (I took off the sunglasses and took off the hoodie). I would love for someone to devise a painless and cost effective way to return my skin back to normal." I stopped talking for a second. "I was about to tell you why I was following you, but you never told me why you were so upset."

"I heard through the grapevine that a friend of mine was killed."

"Who was your friend?"

Tears started to flee from her tear ducts. "Jen Walker."

"Did AJ tell you?"

"Yes, you know AJ?"

"Not personally."

"How did you hear about Jen?"

"Because, dear Jenni, I was the one that killed her, and took out her body parts. That was why I was following you. I am going to do the same to you. I told you I was a humanist. You're young, in reasonably good shape; your grafts will enhance other people's lives. Did you know one full donor, that's where you take almost everything out, can help nearly sixty people?"

"Fuck off!" She tried to spit on me, but by then I had gotten up.

I started draping her for the skin removal. I had all the containers out for her viewing pleasure. She started yelling copious amounts of curse words. I took a piece of tape and put it tightly over her mouth. "Wow, that's better. Those aren't very nice words coming out of your mouth, Jenni. Shame on you! Now it's time to take your skin, Jenni!" I didn't want her to squirm, so for good measure, I punched her in her bloodied face, and stomped on her stomach a few times. Good times, dear readers. Good times.

But by now, you know the deal, folks, on how I removed the skin. It's pointless telling it again and again. However, I would delight in telling you how I removed Jenni's heart.

I must tell you this, from Jenni's lower belly to her feet I had placed a drape and taped it to her sides. Then I had a drape that went over her face and head so only her throat, breasts, and midsection was exposed. I shaved her belly with a sterile disposal razor, and then used a piece of tape I had cut, and tapped it on her stomach to remove any fine hair. I put that in a garbage bag. Jenni fidgeted some as I donned my PPE. I told her to shut the fuck up, or I would really hit her. That did the trick. It was time for me to use the soap in circular motions from the top of her chest down past her sternum, to just above her navel. I won't need to go that far down to remove the heart, but I like my sterility, and I liked looking at her belly. For the removal of hearts, saphenous veins, and skin, the process required different instruments.

I looked at Jenni's imploring eyes. Tears streamed from her face. I had to console her. "Jenni, don't worry. I know it hurts real bad. Don't worry, sweetie. The heart comes out next, but you'll be dead long before I do that." Nope, that didn't do the trick. Maybe I should take some interpersonal communication classes. My bedside manner was terrible.

It was time to take her heart. I took a sterile disposable scalpel blade and made an incision from Jenni's right side on her upper chest, and brought it down, outside of her nipple, and continued down to her diaphragm. I had to be careful not to cut lower as I would slice through the intestines and everything would be contaminated. I continued going around the other side and sliced through her left side and outside her nipple, effectively creating a U-shaped incision.

I carefully placed the scalpel in a Ziploc baggie and took another sterile one. I peeled the skin from the diaphragm up to Jenni's upper chest. I let the skin and adipose fall on her draped face as I retrieved the rib cracker. The rib cutter, or cracker, looked like large wire cutters. I confirmed there wasn't a heartbeat. "Sorry Jenni. You probably were a nice person, but I need some money. Do you know how much money I spend on my mother's alcohol needs? Of course you don't. You just lie there dead, uncaring about my predicament!"

Undeterred, I cut through the ribs along the U shape incision I had made. I heard the ribs go *crack, crack, and crack* as the rib cutters cut through Jenni's ribs like they were paper. Then I lifted the ribs and cartilage as far as I could. I used a few towel clamps and hemostats to pin it to Jenni's flap of skin that rested on his draped face.

Now I had to carefully remove the pericardium, a thin membrane which enveloped the heart. Slice it too deep and it would penetrate the heart, something I didn't want to do. But I was confident; I had taken many hearts out.

I grabbed a pair of sterile forceps, lifted the membrane and carefully sliced through it. I took a pair of mayo's, cut around the heart, and carefully extracted the pericardium, placed it in a sterile bag, tied it and put it in a marked container. I did that as an added bonus for my client. See how nice I am? How I like to help people, and my client? What did I get in return besides money? Nothing! Just people pleading with their miserable lives when they don't comprehend what a miserable life I led!

Sorry, once that was completed, it was time to remove the heart. I put sterile towels on both sides of the victim's lungs to avoid contamination. The heart was usually nestled between the two.

With delicate precision, I reached down into the chest cavity and took the non-beating heart and lifted it into my sterile gloved hands. Tracing the three valves that sat on top of the aortic arch, I grabbed three umbilical cord clamps, and snapped them as far back on the three valves as I could without ripping them. While the chest cavity was full of blood, clamping the valves would ensure no more blood would come out until after I had cut them just in front of the valves where the clamp was inserted. I had known blood would pool in the chest cavity. I brought a few dozen sterile towels, and every once in a while, I had to get them from the sterile field and have the towels absorb the blood since I didn't have any suction equipment with me.

Satisfied, I found the pulmonary artery and clamped it. I did the same process for the inferior vena cava, which was located on the bottom of the heart.

I cut out the heart and placed it over an empty container. I made an incision on the apex, or the top of the heart and poured sodium chloride to clean it. Each company had different solutions which they wanted used to ship it, but in this particular case, since I didn't know what company I was procuring for, I opted to use a solution I used for skin, RPI. It was the wrong solution to keep the heart in, but that's all I had with me.

Now that I was finished, I looked around for the box I usually put my grafts in. Typically, I placed the flattened box inside my oversize jacket, and carried my bag to my side which kept the box in place, but today I forgot. I was in such euphoria about tonight's recovery, it had slipped my mind. I took off my bloodied gown and gloves, walked to the curtains, and moved them to one side about two inches wide. I looked to my left and right. I did not see a soul. I checked the windows of the houses I could see from my vantage point, but could not discern if anyone was looking. Damn, I had to take a calculated risk. I didn't want to take the risk of carrying everything for it to fall out of my hands. If the top opened, and the grafts fell out, they were contaminated.

One time, during the beginning of my tissue procurement career, I had dropped a femur on the floor in a morgue. It was only two seconds on the ground before I scooped it up. I poured bottle and bottles of rubbing alcohol to try to stop anything from growing on it. A few weeks later, I found out they had to throw the thigh bone out, it had been compromised.

So you see, dear readers, my concern for carrying Jenni's skin and heart outside without being in a cardboard box, was justified. I cautiously exited the house without appearing to panic. I tried to make it look like I belonged to the neighborhood. I looked straight ahead, fully confident no one would say anything, or remember me. I got the box, put inside my coat, and walked back to Jenni's house. Easy peasey. I carefully rolled whatever remained of Jenni to one side and pushed the back table cover underneath her. I went to the other side, rolled her slightly the other way, and took hold of the back table cover, and removed it without any of the blood still in the chest cavity, from falling out.

I was about to leave with my bag, the box, and the small garbage bag when I realized I forgot to do something. I put another pair of gloves on, reached inside my jacket pocket, and took out the plastic baggie that housed the strip of tape that held AJ's fingerprints. I put a couple on Jenni's dismembered body, on the door handle, and a couple of places near the body. Satisfied, I walked to my car carrying the cardboard box, got in and drove away. When I was a couple of miles away, I texted (yes, while driving, dear readers) and let the client know I completed the task. I just had to await their reply. God, I loved this line of work!

June 21st

Sorry I have been gone for a while, folks. I contracted a bug that would not leave. I haven't left my room much because I felt drained of energy. Now that I am feeling better, I will relate to you how Detective Jay Club caught me. And if you think that is the end of my story, with me being locked up in an asylum, you would be wrong.

Before I commence, I had to let you know that AJ Mandary was arrested again. This time, because it was his second infraction, I'm not sure he could get out of it. Perhaps if I killed someone again, with the same MO, they would let him go. Or they may think I am a copycat, copying AJ. I am not well versed in law and police procedure.

A while back, in another entry, I related to you how I saw a picture of Detective Jay Club, and his extremely pretty girlfriend, Brittany Schott. Jay said it became personal when I killed his niece, Jen Walker. Why not get more personal than with his girlfriend? I didn't know if Brittany lived with Jay, or owned a separate place. I didn't even know what she did for a living. First things first. I went to the local library instead of my computer because I didn't want any evidence I had done a search on my next victim. Call me paranoid, but my precautions have gotten me this far. I went online, and look her up on social media.

Found out what town she lived in, did a search and came across two different addresses for the same name in the same town. I had to check out both addresses. I wrote down the addresses on a piece of paper and a pen the library supplied. I took the pen, and the small blank pieces of papers that were underneath the paper I wrote the address on. I didn't want any fingerprints, or some smart-ass cop taking a pencil and rubbing it on the paper that was below mine to find the address I had written down. And I didn't want to plug anyone's address in my phone because even if I deleted it, the phone company would still have a record of it.

The first Brittany lived in Noblesville in a neighborhood with a zillion kids playing in the streets. It was late afternoon with the sun shining in my eyes. Even with my sunglasses, I had to put down the visor. I found the address easy enough but I didn't want to overstay my welcome. I slowly drove past her house, and saw two boys playing tag on the lawn. A woman came out with what looked like lemonade. She was tall and blond. Okay, she clearly wasn't the Brittany I was looking for. My Brittany was shorter with long black hair.

The last address was way out in the country, north east of Noblesville. It had some acreage to it. The two-story house was large with four windows on the top floor, and four windows on the first floor. The house was gray, with the door being silver. Odd color scheme but I'm not an interior decorator. The porch extended across the expanse of the front of the house. I drove around the circumference of the property. It took me nearly five minutes to traverse. As I rounded a corner, I saw her coming out her back door. She had long black hair that flew freely in the wind. She was wearing a white t-shirt and blue jean shorts with light blue sneakers. Her socks barely went above her ankles. It would be both a shame and a thrill to kill this woman! Brittany grabbed hold of the garden hose and was watering the garden area. She grew an assortment of vegetables that were enclosed with chicken wire.

I will not lie, dear readers. Unholy thoughts rammed through my brain. But I had to dismiss them immediately. I was procuring her tissue, and did not want to leave any trace of me anywhere. That would spell my doom.

I knew where she lived but didn't know if Jay lived with her. I couldn't park anywhere nearby because she would become suspicious about a lone car parking on the street. I know I would think the same thing. Brittany took out her phone from her back pocket. She read, what I presumed was a text. Damn, I rushed to grab my high-powered binoculars from my backseat. I was able to discern the message. It was from Jay. He said he wouldn't be able to come over.

He was still preoccupied with the serial killer. He wouldn't be over until sometime tomorrow. Brittany texted back she was fine, not to worry about anything. Everything would be all right. No, everything won't be all right Brittany Schott, no it won't.

I took my time pulling away from the curb so no one would notice me. I would come back tonight. Brittany Schott, this will be your last night of your existence on planet Earth. I trembled with delight at the thought of her dying horrifically at my skilled hands.

I texted the client I had another donor available. She would be a full donor, even if the client texted back and told me they only needed certain grafts. *It would not matter to me!* She would be my greatest accomplishment! I would take everything I possibly could, minus the saphenous veins. But I was okay with that.

I pulled in my driveway as the rain started coming down in droves. The weather would not deter my mission! I ran into the house, went into my bedroom, and set my alarm for me to get up in a few hours. I had things to do, and prepare for the culmination of my extracurricular activities. The last thing I thought about before drifting off to sleep was Brittany laying on the floor, nude, and her upper and lower torso were hollowed out.

June 27th

I wanted to let you know what happened to Brittany but I had to have physical therapy since my last entry, and my hands hurt, a lot. So much so, I had almost given up hope. But it was my civic duty to recount the gruesome details of the death of Brittany Schott.

I had woken up to find the rain was still coming down. It was almost nine at night. The cloud cover totally obscured the night sky. I hated the rain, but enjoyed the cloudy night. I went to my medical bag, and took out the instrument cases for skin (dermatome) and bones. They were dirty, and I had to return them to work to have them cleaned, and sterilized in the decontamination room at my job. I went to my closet, and took out a sterile instrument case for skin, bones (tendons included), and heart. I planned on taking Brittany's skin, bones, both upper bones in her arms (Humerus, Ulna, and the Radius), and the lower bones. I was going to take her pericardium, heart, her peritoneal membrane, and just for the fuck of it, her mandible. I knew I had a plastic jawbone that I stole from work somewhere around here. I searched all of the shelves in my closet, and finally found it hidden underneath some sterile glove packs. It was kind of big, probably meant for a male, but I would shove that bad boy in Brittany's mouth after her mandible was removed, and force it in there, then suture her mouth shut. I loved when I sounded forceful!

It was still early; I had wanted to get there around eleven. After finding all of the instruments, and packing everything, it was only nine thirty. I would get there at ten. Oh well, an hour early just meant Brittany had one less hour to live. I walked with my gear to the car, put my stuff in my in the backseat, and drove to her house. With the darkness now upon me, and the rain clouding everyone's vision that drove, I was positive I would remain unseen. This time, I wouldn't park in the street. I would use the back entrance I had noticed when I surveyed her house.

I arrived a little after ten, with my heart racing, and I had butterflies in my stomach. When I got near Brittany's back entrance, I turned off my lights, and drove all the way to the large barn that was behind her house. The rain continued unabated, and the clouds remained. I was going to walk to the house but I decided I wanted to see what was in her barn. As I walked to the barn, I noticed I had stepped in mud from all of the rain. After I killed Brittany, I would have to figure out a way to get rid of my shoe prints, and my tire prints as well. Maybe Brittany would know what to do. I would have to ask her. She seemed the helpful type. Although, my other victim, Andre King, never gave me any financial advice. Some help he was.

I couldn't see much through the dirty windows. I didn't want to rub the glass even though I had gloves on. Call me obsessed. I did manage to see a long work bench made of plywood, with lots of tools, and a vice grip at the end that was attached to the work bench. The floor was concrete, with light brown barrels of varying sizes. A riding lawn mower, some rakes, several concrete blocks, and a plethora of other garden tools. So Brittany liked to work with her hands. So did I! It was a commonality that must be mentioned. I walked toward the house, passing my car along the way. The mud made sucking noises when my shoes went up and down as I walked closer and closer to Brittany's back door. On more than one occasion, I thought my shoes had come off. I was going to rehearse what to say. Initially I was going to tell Brittany my car had broken down, but with the rain, I nixed that idea. Then I would have to do the old standby, the element of surprise. I went to her back door and put my ear to the window. I didn't hear any dogs. I hope she didn't have any dogs when I pounced on her. I noticed she had a back light that was turned off. I unscrewed the light bulb just enough to keep it in place, but far enough out where the light wouldn't come on. I knocked gingerly on her wooden door. It was now or never. My heart was pumping, and adrenaline was coursing through my veins!

A few seconds later, I heard someone walking.

Her back door led to her kitchen, and she was entering it from another room. She did not turn on the kitchen light, which was odd. Maybe she intended to turn on the outside light. She had a remote in her hand. She must have been watching TV.

She did not open the door. Not what I expected. "Can I help you?" She said through the door's window. I could tell she was trying to turn the light switch on a few times, and was confused why it wouldn't come on. I had taken a few steps back where it was a little darker.

Maybe the car trick would work after all. I took a look at the street and was happy to note, you couldn't see it that clearly. Additionally, dear readers, she couldn't see my car parked next to her barn until she walked around the house. "I am having car trouble, and was wondering if I could use your cell phone to call my girlfriend. Sorry, but I am drenched, and I think my battery died, and I am tired."

Once I mentioned another female, her features softened. She opened the door, and let me in. "I think cars are the bane of society," Brittany remarked.

"I agree. Thank you for letting me in."

"Let me get my phone, it's just around the corner."

I hoped she wasn't getting her gun. That would tend to ruin the evening I had planned. But as luck would have it, she brought the phone I had seen her use earlier in the day. She handed it to me. As I was about to take hold of it, I purposely let it slip from my hands. I watched her eyes dart to her phone, and judged if she would be able to grab it before it smashed on the ground. That was my cue. While she was distracted, I punched her in the face. She staggered back, but did not fall. Huh, everyone else fell, even Andre, and he was tall! Before she had a chance to realize what was going on, I rushed her, and pushed her into the kitchen wall, well away from the knives I had noticed. Her head snapped against the wall, but she still wasn't out of commission. I punched her in the face again, and then punched her in the stomach. It took the wind out of her. However, I didn't trust going to my car to get my stuff while she was still able to fight back. She was holding her stomach when I punched her in the face. Her hands went to her face, so I punched her in the stomach again. You'd think she would know what was coming next, but she didn't. I was thinking, Jesus, Brittany, fall down! She was leaning against the wall, and slowly used her back to go down, albeit slow. I grabbed her long, dark hair, and dragged her to the room adjacent to the kitchen. Her fingers were trying to dig into my hands as clumps of her hair were being removed as I shifted positions whenever she tried to scratch me. It was a large living room with hardwood floors. A white three-piece sofa set was in the center with a large curio cabinet to one side with dishes and plates on the shelves.

I noticed she was watching one of those game shows where the answer came first, and then you had to ask the question. The enormous Mahogany coffee table had paper and a pen. I checked what she had written. She was keeping score of how many she had gotten correct. Smart girl. I grasped her head and smashed it against the coffee table a few times. She fell to the floor, unconscious. Finally! Man, was she resilient! I checked my hands. Blood was coming from several places. That meant she had my blood under her fingernails. Nope, couldn't have that.

I couldn't risk going outside and get my stuff if she would come to. I saw some of her light fixtures were strung up with wire, and hung down from the ceiling. That would have to do. But first, I closed the curtains. I knew I was in a remote part of town, but you never knew if someone would ride by, and call the police.

I shoved the coffee table underneath the hanging lamps, stood up and pulled on the wire. They were attached pretty well. I had to look for something to dislodge them. I walked just past Brittany when she grabbed my ankle, and I fell. I didn't have my cattle prod or any other weapon on me. Everything was in the car. She got on top of me, effectively locking my arms in place, and took my hoodie and sunglasses off, and gasped. "You! Jay told me there were reports of someone going around skinning people alive, and taking out their body parts!" I noticed her forehead was red from the coffee table.

"What are you talking about? How does he know it's me?"

"The cameras at the mall made them suspicious when they traced Jen Walker's movements, and saw the two shouting matches you had with her. Then someone at the liquor store called the police but you were gone by the time they arrived! They know about your mustard colored skin from you ID!" She started slapping me, hard. She had my arms pinned beneath her, so I was defenseless. You may say, dear readers that I deserved what I was getting. But nothing could be further then the truth. Her body parts were going to enhance more lives than just hers. How selfish on her part! Her slaps slowly died down as she started breathing heavier. The beating was pale compared to the ones I was afflicted with for so long.

I started pushing my hips in the air, trying to force her off me. When I pushed my hips up the last time, I felt my hands were able to move a little. I pinched the jeans on her legs as hard as I could. She screamed in pain, and flew off me. I only had one chance at this because we were both tuckered. We got up and faced each other. We were about six or seven feet apart. Brittany tried the element of surprise on me. On me, that was a good one. Without warning, which I figured she would do, she came at me running and screaming. Just before she got to me I pivoted, put my leg out, and Brittany tripped over it. She fell to the floor face first. I seized the moment. I put my knee into her spine, and dug in. I took her head, and rammed it into the hardwood flooring over a dozen times. That had to hurt. Not that I felt sorry for her. She was the first person who actually fought back. Jay would have been proud of her.

I looked around and saw my shoe prints all over the house. Damned mud. It would take me a few hours to clean the mess up. What was this, amateur hour? Better get to work!

I turned Brittany over on her back. I smacked her in the face really hard to see if she was out, or if she came to. Nothing. Either she was a good actor, or she was out cold. I could not take the chance. The hanging lamps were out. Too much work to get them down. I scanned the room I was in, and the adjourning room. The house wasn't entirely dark, but most of the lights were off. The only handy item I saw, which I didn't want to use, but had to until I came back from my car was the tablecloth. I had two options with that.

One of the tablecloths was from the dining room, and the dining room table was humongous. That left the kitchen table. It was big, but not nearly as long as the dining room tablecloth. I ran full speed into the kitchen, grabbed the tablecloth, and yanked. The basket of fruits, along with a napkin holder full of napkins, fell to the floor. I swung the tablecloth around by both ends to make it thinner, and compact. Thankfully Brittany was still lying there. To make sure she wasn't faking it again, I kicked her hard in her side. Nothing. I took the tablecloth, and tied up her hands and feet together. She was hog tied. But, when I left, if she came to, she would be able to scream. Not a neighbor for a few miles, but I didn't want to take the chance.

Brittany's house was large, and I didn't have the time to search every room for something to stuff in her mouth. Nevertheless, I figured the bedrooms were upstairs. I ran up the stairs, taking two at a time. I got up to the top and there were two long hallways to choose from. Brittany was sure making it more difficult for me. I ran to the nearest bedroom, and looked through all of her dresser drawers, nothing. The next two bedrooms yielded the same result. Where the hell was her bedroom? At the fourth bedroom, I found a more lived in room. I scoured her dresser drawer, and found her socks were just above her panty drawer. Hmm, which one to stuff in her mouth? You guessed it, her panties. Fuck her, she tried to incapacitate me! I was about to leave when I passed her adjacent bathroom. On the counter were several colors of nail polish, nail polish remover, a nail file, and a pair of clippers. I grabbed the clippers.

I ran downstairs to where she still lay. She was struggling to free herself but with her hands and feet tied together, she wasn't going anywhere. "Hi Brittany, miss me?"

"Fuck you, freak! When Jay gets here, he's going to murder you! He will..."

I shoved both of her pink panties in her pretty mouth. She was still talking. I kicked her hard in her side a few times. That did the trick. "Brittany, honey, I saw the text Jay sent you, and your response. He won't be here until sometime tomorrow. Relax; I have plenty of time to play with you." I smacked her in the back of her head a few times. "I have to go to my car to get a few things. Don't go anywhere, okay?" I made sure the knots were tight, and to make sure she wouldn't try to crawl on her belly, I dragged her by her hair and stopped near the couch. I had about a foot and a half excess tablecloth left, and tied it around the sofa's leg. Hopefully she wouldn't be stronger than what the couch weighed.

I went outside in the downpour, and realized I

still had to contend with the mud, but I needed my equipment to complete the job. I opened my car door, got what I needed, and ran back to Brittany's house. When I went to the living room, she was still there, cursing. She started to struggle when I went to her. I untied the tablecloth from the sofa leg, and using her legs, dragged her to the middle of the room where there was less light, but illuminated enough for me to procure. I grabbed her hips and pivoted her over on her back. Now she was looking up at me. She was still cursing at me. Before any procurement, I make sure I wore gloves. Always. While she was still mumbling colorful metaphors at me, I took my gloved hand and put it to her moist lips. "Shh... Brittany. Shut the fuck up!" She tried to bite my finger even though her mouth was stuffed. I took clear packing tape from my medical bag, and put a piece over her mouth. Then I took out my cattle prod. Her eyes bulged from their sockets when she recognized what was headed toward her. She tried even harder to free herself as the prod descended down to her shoulder, then the other shoulder. Then in-between her chest, and slowly made my way down her belly. Then her inner thighs, all the way down her legs. That calmed her down. She moaned in pain. While her body revolted, I untied the tablecloth. Shit and piss came streaming out. Fuck! I moved her toward the wall, away from the curtains. I wedged her body between a recliner, and an oversize love seat.

"Are you done voiding?" I asked sarcastically. No response. I used rope to tie her hands to the recliner, and her feet to the love seat. Now came fun time!

I waited about five minutes for any residual convulsions to stop. Before I set up the sterile field, I wanted to have some fun. I slapped her until her eyes came into focus. When she woke up, I realized something. I didn't want to do the slicing and dicing here in her house. All the people I killed didn't have a huge barn in their backyard. I'm sure there were tools I could use to play with Brittany. But the muck and mud! I didn't want to drag her by her hair or her feet through it. I wanted sterile body parts, not dirty ones. I thought about keeping her here in the house, but the barn held some allure for me, dear readers. Years later, I still regretted that fateful and rash decision. If I had kept Brittany inside, well... you'll see why soon enough.

Fortunately, I had not stripped her down. Her hands and feet were still tied together with the tablecloth while facedown. I untied the cloth which bound the hands to her feet. Before this woman could move a muscle, I tied her hands up tight with rope I had found in my medical bag. I reached into my bag again, withdrew a sharp pair of scissors, and cut the cloth around her legs. I put the scissors back in my bag, and tied her legs up with the excess rope. I was going to kill this woman tonight if it was the last thing I do!

That being done, I yanked her up by her long dark hair. I had made sure there was ample room for Brittany to walk, but not to run.

Brittany was mumbling something but I wasn't about to take off the tape and remove her panties from her mouth. "I am assuming you want to know where we're going, right? I thought you might like a change in scenery. How about the barn?" She turned her head back and forth vigorously. She tried to stop while I was taunting her. "Stop being a big baby, Brittany! It's not like you're going to be awake while I remove your skin, and the rest of you." I snapped my fingers while I kept pushing her forward. "Oh, wait a second. Yes, yes, you'll be awake. Totally awake. My bad."

I pushed her to the back door. I turned around and saw the mud mess I had created. It was either clean up, or buy a new pair of totally different shoes. Luckily those shoes were bought with cash a long time ago. It had to have been at least five, six years ago. Although, I would feel obligated to clean the mud prints. After all, who wants mud, coupled with potential evidence, on their floors? Am I right? I think so!

Opening the back door proved difficult with

Brittany wiggling and being difficult. "Brittany, will you relax? You might fall and hurt yourself!" I had to laugh at the irony of my statement. But if she did fall and break a bone or two that was one less graft I would get to take out. I had to calm the woman down. I put my hand to the back of her head, and shoved it into the back door. Her face hit the wood molding that kept the glass from falling out. She was still squirming. God this woman was feisty! I pushed her a few feet to the right of the door, and then shoved her head a few times into the wall. Finally, she was too dazed to try her shenanigans. I forcefully led her to the barn, right around the corner. On the backside of the house, no cars were able to see me or Brittany. It took only a couple of minutes to get to the barn. I tried to turn the handle, something I didn't attempt earlier, and it was locked. "Where's the key, bitch?"

Brittany's hair was soaked, as was everything else. She tried to smile but the packing tape held her mouth in place. "Oh, you're going to be like that, are ya?" I pushed her to the wall, not far from the door, and turned her so she faced me. I wanted this woman facing me while I thought what to do. I checked my watch and was amazed over an hour had elapsed, and I hadn't even started the procurement. That was definitely strange. I hope my delay wasn't ominous. In the end, it took me five tries to kick in the door. I pushed her in, and kicked her behind her knee. She fell to the ground on her knees. I pushed her down so her face was to the concrete. I tried to close the back door but it was too jacked up. I looked around for a piece of two by four to hold the door in place, so it would serve as a deterrent if someone tried to come in. I found one lying in the corner of the room. Before I put it in place, I realized my bag and equipment was still in the house. Okay, no problem. On the long plywood work bench, I saw some rope. Brittany was still lying on the concrete floor. I rushed to the work bench, grabbed the rope, and hurried back. There were four cinder blocks lined up near the rider lawn mower I saw earlier. Hurriedly, I brought the cinder blocks close to Brittany's non-moving form. I put one on top of the other, then laced a knot through the bottom cinder block, then tied that rope around Brittany's neck and throat. That should keep her stationary.

The run to her house exhilarated me. The adrenaline that was coursing through me should help me when the time comes with Brittany. It took only a few minutes to pack everything back up and bring them to the barn. After I closed the barn's door, I put the two by four in place, up against the door. Now, it was just Brittany and me. I could hear the rain patter against the windows. It was the only noise present. I was silent listening to the rain beat against the building too. It was calming. I don't know how long I was in la la land until I came out of it. As I've stated previously, I had a tendency to do that.

I walked over to Brittany, and she was still not moving. I didn't trust her. Would you, dear readers? I kicked her hard in the leg, and she made a feeble attempt to come at me. The rope on her neck stopped her from looking up too much. "I knew you were faking it, Brittany. You're a smart one, I'll give you that. Did you want me to chat with you while I create the sterile field?" I looked at her, she nodded her head no. "Cool, I thought you might! So, at this point you might be asking yourself, Brittany, what body parts is this guy going to take from me? Just about everything." Her eyes widened, and creases erupted on her forehead. I stopped what I was doing, went to her, and knelled beside her. "You don't have to worry honey; you'll be dead after a few bones are removed. It's not like you have a say, or you're doing any of the work! Of course, I am doing everything, like always! All you have to do is lie there and look pretty! Do you know how hard it is for me to set up a procurement? No, you don't! I have to do all of the leg work, and the reconnaissance! How about the gas money? Are you going to pay me for that? Huh? Are you?" I got mad, stood up abruptly, and I stomped on her right arm. I regretted it right after my foot was raised, and before it came crashing down on Brittany's Humerus bone (Dear readers, the Humerus is the arm bone that goes from the shoulder to the elbow). I heard the snap, crackle, and pop almost immediately. Damn! What did I do? I could take the Ulna and the Radius (the arm bones from the elbow to the wrist) from both sides, and the Humerus from the left side, but I'm a stickler for removing the best grafts, and tried hard to bring the client two of everything that could be taken out. I made an executive decision. I was going to forgo the arm bones because of my foolishness! "Sorry Brittany! I have been under a lot of strain lately. Actually, my whole life. But recently, I've been feeling a bit more stressed. Maybe it's the thrill of the chase, the procurement of body parts on my off days, my mother being a pain in the ass. You get the picture, don't you?"

I heard whimpering. Poor girl was crying. She must be in a great deal of pain. I thought about consoling her, dear readers. After all, after taking her skin, and all of her lower tendons and bones, she would be dead already. Even if she wasn't, it wouldn't be long from there. But I could not work up the empathy to calm her. So, I decided to get to work. I put the back table covers on the floor, not far from the crybaby. There was a couple of low to the ground, beaten up coffee tables near the back of the place. I brought those over, and covered them to create the sterile field to put my supplies.

I took out my supplies, and changed my gloves,

because as I stated previously, I always wore gloves, and took out the instruments. I carefully laid everything out, donned my PPE, and was ready to commence the procedure. By the looks of things, crybaby wasn't ready. I let out a great deal of air to calm myself, then bent down on the back table cover, took a firm grasp of Brittany flesh, and rolled her on her back. Thankfully, I put a few covers down, so I had room to play before anything was outside of the sterile field. That would be a no-no. Her eyes were shut and she managed to grimace, but I choose to ignore it.

I slapped her hard across her face several times before she would open her eyes. "Hey brat, you know what you are? You're a party pooper, that's what you are, Brittany! Look at all the trouble I went through for you! Do you realize what all of this planning entailed? No! Of course not! You're too selfish." I waited for a response of any kind. Nothing. Figures. "Okay, that's how you want to play it, huh? I can play it that way too!"

I removed the rope from around Brittany's neck from the cinder blocks, carefully so the blocks wouldn't touch the sterile gown I had on. I put one block next to each of Brittany's hands, and the same for the feet. Don't worry, dear readers, I put them well outside of the sterile field.

I cut rope that I took from the top of the long work bench into four pieces. I tied each piece to a cinder block, and then, not thinking, cut the ropes from Brittany's hands, and tied them up from the cinder block rope. I did the same thing for the feet. What was I thinking? I just contaminated the whole sterile field! Was this amateur night again? I counted to twenty-five to calm myself, then I laid out a few more back table covers on the still sterile coffee tables, then I took off my PPE, put on sterile gloves, grabbed the covers, and knelt beside Brittany, raised her to one side, pushed the covers underneath her, then went to the other side, raised her to the side, and took out the cover. I got up, took off the gloves, and put more covers on the floor. I put new PPE's on, and then felt reasonably comfortable it would be smooth sailing from there. I should ask for hazard pay from the client.

"Brittany, are you awake?" No response. "Hey! Wake up! Do not pretend to be dead when I haven't even started!" Instead of slapping or punching her, I casually knelt to the side of her, and started unbuttoning her shirt. That woke her up. Her eyes bulged out of her head. I made her legs outstretched as far as I could with the ropes. The arms were outstretched, even the broken one, so she wouldn't be able to move much. I unbuttoned the last button, reached into my bag, took out my scissors, and cut the sleeves so the shirt would be totally off her. I cut her bra off, traced my finger down her midsection, and then reached for her button to her jeans, all the while looking at her pleading eyes. It was difficult removing her pants and panties because she refused to cooperate. Since the shirt, pants and panties weren't sterile; I took gloves off, put fresh ones on. Dear readers, I am constantly telling you I put sterile gloves on, then off, then on. I do it not out of repetition, but for your knowledge I did everything possible to maintain sterility.

I had time to kill, and it being a nice night, I laid down beside her. I looked at the ceiling. "I bet I can see pictures on the ceiling! Can you?" She looked over at me like I was nuts. "I see the shape of Godzilla's head, do you?" I pointed to the middle of the ceiling where the light reflected a certain way. She refused to look. Breaking the ice wasn't my strong suit. I went back to kneeling. Maybe if I shared a secret with her, she would stop thinking about her broken arm, or the fact I was going to mutilate her. After all, I told the prostitute stuff I haven't told anybody, I tried to get Andre King to give me financial advice. Jen Walker and I talked about the norms of society. Why not Brittany? It helped create a connection, right dear readers?

"Brittany, I am going to let you on a secret that no one knows, okay? Well one of my victims knew, but now that person is dead, so technically, no one knows but me. You know what my favorite part of a woman is, besides the obvious boobs, vagina, ass, and lips are? You'd probably be surprised; it's a woman's belly. Silly, right? Who the hell cares about women's bellies? I care!" I yelled at her while I took of my sterile gloves. I now had my bare hands. I traced my fingers down her soft belly, stopping at her belly button. I grabbed both sides of her belly button, and squeezed tightly. "I don't really care for skinny girls, or obese girls, no offense to them, Brittany. I like a woman with some soft flesh, ya know, some meat on them. That is not implying you're fat, because sweet Jesus, you're not!" I took my fist and slowly, but deeply, punched her in her tummy as far in as it would go. Then I did it harder. Feeling that flesh envelope my fist was awesomeness! The only thing that would have made it better was if she were into it too. I saw the pained expression on her face, and that excited me. But... like I stated before, I wasn't here to leave my DNA, so reluctantly I took some pairs of sterile gloves, but seeing her lying there helpless, and her body exposed, before I put the gloves back on, I had to do it more time. When she wasn't expecting it, so the stomach muscles weren't tightened, I punched her in the softest part of her abdomen, held it there for fifteen, twenty seconds, and brought my fist up.

"Okay Brittany, it's time." Before I started on any body part, I took the clippers, and grabbed hold of her fingers. One by one I removed the entire nail from each finger. I may have cut too far down on most of them that produced a lot of blood, but there was no way I was leaving any DNA!

Now, dear readers, I have already described how to take the skin, bones, saphenous veins, the pericardium, and the heart. I don't want to bore you with the redundant details. However, I haven't described how to remove the peritoneal membrane or the mandible.

The peritoneal membrane has several functions. I am not going to get technical in case laypeople decided to read my journal. One of its main function is it helps insulate, cushion, and protect the abdominal Organs.

I had placed a sterile drape several inches below her navel and one covering her chest. After using soap, I took a sterile scalpel, and cut into the flesh just below her rib cage on one side, went down, but not too far down, then cut down to a couple of inches below her belly button. I did the same for the other side. I started humming a song from childhood. I saw her scrunched up face, obviously in pain. Wrinkles deepened on her forehead, her eyes were shut. She should be enjoying the experience! Oh well, her loss. Then going to the point of incision, I cut horizontally until my blade met the other side's incision. I did the same for below the belly button. Essentially, dear readers, I cut a decent sized square. I changed blades, then took a mayo, grabbed the flesh, then cut underneath, avoiding the intestines. I made sure as I pulled the membrane that nothing but the skin and adipose went with it. The procedure took a while but it was worth it. The sound the flesh makes as its being peeled and removed are equal to a composer creating a masterpiece. It's akin to bacon being slowly cooked on a skillet, only the noise was a little softer.

After I diligently removed the membrane, and put it in the marked baggie, I took the time to check out her intestines. They were so soft and gooey in my hands. I played with them for a few minutes, basking in the glory of the procurement. Later on, when I will have to stitch her up, the peritoneal membrane would take some time. In essence, I would have to find her belly button, and line up the skin so all the square pieces of the skin would look aesthetically pleasing. Never let it be said that Ben Berstgel wasn't diligent with his suture skills to make my victims look more comfortable.

But before that came the mandible, or the jawbone. Again, I cleaned the area using 4% CHG after I placed a sterile cover on Brittany's throat down to her exposed intestines. Then I placed a drape just below her nose, and put it over her head. I took my scalpel right where the bone meets the ear. I made an incision there, and then carefully cut where the outline of Brittany's jaw line was until it met the other ear. Then I cut the tendons that kept the mandible in place near both ears. Using a pair of mayos, I surgically peeled the skin with the help of the scalpel. After that process was completed, I took the excess skin from her jaw, and pulled it up over on to Brittany's face so just the mandible was visible. I twisted the mandible until the mandible came loose, and eventually came out. I had brought a plastic one to replace her real one, but I looked at it. It was way too big for Brittany's mouth.

Unfortunately, Brittany lost her life somewhere between removing the tibula, taking the mallet and chisel, and hammering the hip bone loose enough until I was able to twist it free from the attached muscle. She was a real trooper. I daresay I will miss her. She was my toughest opponent yet.

And then, dear readers, all hell broke loose. Right now, the incident was dredging up bad memories. I need a break.

July 7[h]

Folks, I needed several days recuperation from what I had told you about in the last entry. You might ask why, and that would be a reasonable question. The last thing I ever expected happened. Detective Jay Club started pounding on the door of the barn. The two by four wouldn't hold him long, especially once he saw what I had done to Brittany. I took off my face mask, and the top pair of gloves, but kept the scalpel as Jay barged in.

Jay had the nerve to aim his gun at my head. "Is she dead? Because if she's dead, you're not walking out of here alive," he said with conviction.

I refused to answer him because I thought the answer was obvious.

"Is she fucking dead?!" Jay yelled at the top of his lungs. The sound of Jay's anger reverberated across the room. Good acoustics, I thought.

I bent down to where Brittany's lifeless form was sprawled. I picked up her head, looked down at her, and let her head fall back down to the ground. I could tell the amount of blood on the back table covers, and my gown, appalled Jay.

"I would have to say yes, she is definitely dead, Jay."

"Move away from her, you piece of shit!"

I did as he instructed.

"You do know I am going to shoot you, right?" Jay declared.

"Why on earth would you shoot me, Jay? Just because I killed your niece and girlfriend? Don't make it personal. Do you know how many potential people the two of them might save?"

"I don't give a flying fuck who they might save. No one is going to save you!"

The Detective obviously couldn't grasp the concept I was trying to convey. Jay was a little taller than me, and had me by thirty or more pounds. But he didn't lift corpses, or drag bodies around like I did on an almost daily basis. And if you add my anger issues from my upbringing into the equation, I had a pretty good chance of escaping. The only thing blocking me was his gun. "You know Jay, your niece, Jen Walker, had a gun too. But I still managed to evade her. The same will be applicable with you."

An evil smile surfaced on his face. I really thought he was going to pull the trigger right there. "Freak, the only thing you'll evade tonight is jail time because I am going to shoot you."

There you had it, folks. I tried to reason with him, make him see my point of view. And what did he do? He insulted me! "Jay, calling me a freak was rude. I demand an apology."

"Oh, did I hurt the prissy girl's feelings? Too bad!" He had his gun aimed at my head as he moved closer and closer. Soon, he was barely three feet away from me. But I wasn't backing down. Folks, do you know how much money I would lose if Jay got his way, and I died? A lot! But I was curious about something.

"Jay, you weren't supposed to come here until tomorrow! Why are you here now? I didn't invite you to this procurement."

His gun never wavered as he said, "How did you know about that? Wait, never mind. You probably checked her message on her phone earlier. I called several times later to let her know I was coming over. I needed some time off this case. Brittany always had her phone on her. After the tenth time I called her to let her know I was on my way, I had a gut instinct that something was wrong. I went into her house, and saw your mud tracks, and followed them to the barn."

"Speaking of guts Jay, while her guts were still inside her body, I took out the lining that protects them. It's called the peritoneal membrane. Then I played with her guts, you know, her intestines? The soft gooey feeling is indescribable, Jay. "

"Why you piece of shit!" Jay yelled while he came inches closer.

The conversation wasn't going anywhere, and I didn't know how much time I had left before he actually shot me. "I think you should put your gun down, and provide ample room for me to leave." When he looked at me incredulously, I decided it was time for me to strike first. With sudden ferociousness, I ran to Jay and tackled him. When we hit the ground Jay's hand that was carrying the gun hit the cement first and dislodged it from his grasp. The gun skidded on the concrete floor several yards away. I proved lucky. I still managed to hold on to the scalpel blade. I struck Jay deep into his chest and abdomen several times before he was able to get back up, and back away. Jay took off his coat and saw his white shirt turn red. I sensed his hesitancy and struck again.

Jay was dazed but was able to deflect my swinging scalpel by using his arm. The blade swooped down on his arm and a large tear produced more blood. He looked at the large laceration on his arm, and then looked at me. He knew I had the upper hand. During our confrontation, we had moved away from our original position. The gun was too far for Jay to try to grab. Jay looked around frantically while

I was jumping up and down with joy. I would pretend to strike him, and would laugh when Jay would duck or jump back. "I must say I am surprised and disappointed in your fighting skills, Jay" I said with amusement.

It appeared Jay was getting desperate. He looked around, and I knew why. He was looking for any tools he could use to counter my scalpel blade since the gun was still too far away. "Any last words before I kill you, Jay?" See dear readers, I was polite to him despite his rudeness.

"I'm not one for speeches so give it your best shot, punk," Jay said. I think he spoke with more confidence than he felt.

"I respect your false bravado, Jay. I'll think of you often, and maybe from time to time come and visit your grave. I may even put some flowers on it. How does that sound?"

Jay was leaning against the plywood table. Blood soaked his shirt. He was nearly out of breath, and his face was pale. "It sounds delusional but that's par for the course."

He was goading me. I knew he was dear readers. Why else would he be so disrespectful? I lunged at the Detective but Jay had more in him then he let on. I was about to pounce on him when he moved at the last second, and my blade embedded itself in the plywood.

"My turn!" He took hold of my head and slammed it down with his waiting knee. The effect was immediate. As I went down, I tried to grasp the blade, but Jay wasn't finished with me yet. The tip of the scalpel blade had broken off from my attempt, and Jay kicked it across the room. He was barely able to pick me up from the ground. We stood face to face with him. "This one's for Jen!" He punched me in the face. "This one's for Brittany!" Jay said as he pummeled my face onto the work bench. I could taste blood in my mouth. But he wasn't done, dear readers. No, far from it. He took my head, put my mustard discoloration side on the plywood table top, and shoved my face along the plywood. I could feel splinters digging in my face. On the way back, he took my other side of my face and repeated it. A great deal of the splinters were embedded into my skin! "You were good at scaring people, right? Well, let's make sure you can never frighten anyone again," Jay said with vehemence in his voice.

"Let's talk about this, Jay!" I implored.

He reached across to the pegboard that was on the wall the plywood workbench was against and grabbed plastic ties. He had the nerve to tie my hands together! He dragged my head across the wood table (again!) until he got to the vice grip. More splinters if that was possible!

"How about I put your head in the vice grip?" Jay asked menacingly.

I started pleading with him. "Please Jay; don't put my head in the vice! Please don't. I have enough wrong with me!"

"Is that what the innocent people told you? Did they plead with you and you ignored them too?"

"But I was only trying to help other less fortunate people, Jay!" That was true, but I wasn't going to tell him I enjoyed it too.

He looked at me for a long moment. I could tell he was still bleeding. What was keeping him alive? Sheer determination? He looked me over with ragged breaths. "Tell you what... I won't put your head in the vice grip... after all." He turned around and spit blood on the concrete floor.

My body relaxed. Good, Jay wasn't going to kill me! Maybe I would get out of here unscathed.

"But... what I will do is make you change your... occupation," he said with uneven breath.

I was confused. "What do you mean by that, Jay?"

He took firm hold of my tied hands, put them in the open vice grip and started tightening it. I realized his intention, and tried to pull away. Jay elbowed me in the face a few times. There wasn't much force behind the blows, but it did its job. As the vice grip closed on my hands, I could still vividly recall my screams grew louder and louder until it was a deafening roar. But Jay refused to stop. Finally, my shrieking subsided. I fell to the ground on my knees with my hands still inside the vice grip. I still was coherent enough to deduce Jay was not going to let me out anytime soon. Jay was groggy, but managed to make a phone call. He walked to where Brittany's lifeless body was, and fell. If I had been able to, I would have taken a picture of the two of them lying side by side. How romantic.

The rest was a blur. I was put in prison in solitary confinement until I was made to take some tests, and was sent to the insane asylum in McCordsville, where I currently reside. If that was the end of the story, then Karma wouldn't have had its say.

July 13th

Dear readers, the story of my humble beginning to my subsequent and harrowing capture was over two years ago. Every day I wake up and see the disfigurement of my once skilled hands. I am no longer on the top of the world. That distinction now belonged to Mr. Orderly. He ruled with an iron fist over mine, and everyone else's lives. That was, until recently, true. Now I must recount a few odd happenings here at the sanatorium. I know you picked up this book for entertainment, and excitement, but I still want to give you some background on me. It's still all about me, dear readers, and don't forget that!

I was sleeping when I heard a knock on my door. Since Mr. Orderly doesn't knock, I knew with certainty it wasn't him. I peered at the clock on my nightstand. It was three thirty in the afternoon. Who could that be? Someone knocked again. It wasn't a hesitant knock, it was with force. I rose without conviction before putting my slippers on. By the time I got to the door, the person was knocking again.

There wasn't a peep hole on the door so I had to open it. A strange woman barged in, and walked to the small table where my computer sat. She was of average height with long, brownish red hair that was hung loosely. Her gray sweater hung past her knees and she had a belt that hung loosely around her waist.

She took my laptop off my table, and threw it on my bed. She took the briefcase she was holding, put her hand inside, and withdrew some paperwork. All that took only a few seconds. She turned around and faced me, smiling. She had crooked teeth, with a large forehead. Her blue eyes were spaced too far apart. Her dark eyebrows were shaven, and drawn on. She sat down.

"Who the hell are you?"

"I am Chelst Johnson, and today is your lucky day!"

"How did you get past security?"

"I paid them off."

"Money doesn't work on the guards, I've tried."

"Who said anything about money?"

I put up my contorted hands to let her know I didn't want to hear anymore. It was bad enough I got a visual with her and Mr. Orderly having sex because after security, you had to go through him for anything else. I almost threw up. "What do you want, Chelst?"

"Here is a contract I want you to sign. Come here, read it, then sign it."

Intrigued, even though I had no intention to sign anything, I walked to the table, sat down, and read. I am a quick reader, and finished a few minutes later. "You're an editor? I don't understand. What have I written that would require an editor?"

The chipper lady peered at me. I could smell something foul coming off this woman. I didn't know if it was her lack of hygiene, or what she was trying to sell. "I was told, by a reliable source, you're writing a journal about your exploits for the world to read. Am I right? Am I right? Am I right?

"No, no, and no. Now get your ass out of here. I don't have any money for an editor."

Chelst smiled again. "You don't need any money. We can come to a mutual understanding, if you know what I mean!" She winked at me. Gross.

"I don't need nor do I want, an editor. Now please go."

"Okay, if relations won't work on you, how about you just let me edit your book for a percentage."

"What part of the word no do you not understand? I can't simplify it anymore."

"You're such a dick, you know that?"

"I've been called worse. Not really worried about your opinion of me."

"I'm going to tell Mr. Orderly on you! Hope you like his visit tonight!" She stormed out of my room, and bumped into a man I've never seen before. He was my height, bald, with a goatee that was red. The guy looked her over, turned her around, and kicked her in her ass. "Get back to your room, Chelst!" She didn't budge.

"You can't talk to me like that!" Chelst said between clenched teeth.

"Oh yeah?" The gentleman turned her around to face the hallway, and pushed her into the wall outside of my door. Blood flew freely from her nose, and left residue on the wall. "I'm telling on you!"

The guy walked into my room and closed the door. "Who the fuck was she, and who are you?" I demanded.

The guy smiled. "Her name was Chelst Johnson, and she is a patient here."

"I've never seen her before," I remarked.

"That's because we don't allow you unfettered access. She was admitted recently. Today, she thought she was an editor. A few days ago, she was an aspiring actress. Before that, she was an auto mechanic. She swore up and down she could fix any car, any make, and any model."

"I've already lost interest. Who are you?"

"I am your good fortune, Ben."

"Fortunes are made, and then lost. I am the latter one."

"While that is true, fortune can be attained again."

"I'm sorry, I didn't catch your name," I said with hesitancy.

"My name is Greg Hebert. I'd shake your hand, but..."

"Funny, Greg, really funny. How did you get past Mr. Orderly?"

"That prick got fired. Upper management found out what he was doing to patients, including you."

"Why would upper management care what some nut case did to criminally insane people at a nuthouse? Don't get me wrong; I'm glad he's gone, I just don't understand why."

"Their reputations, Ben. But that's not all the

news I have for you."

"Please, do enlighten me," I said with sarcasm.

Greg walked right up to me. We were within inches of each other. "Enough with the caustic remarks, Ben. I am telling you out of respect."

"Okay. But respect me? You don't even know me."

Greg seemed to ignore my response. "Your Mr. Orderly was found dead at his home, details are sketchy."

"Murdered? Cool! I mean what a shame. They don't think I had anything to do with it, do they?"

"No, you're confined here, and your hands are useless. Plus the manner in which he was killed wasn't your M.O. He was chopped into little pieces. Motive is now being investigated."

"It couldn't have happened to a nicer fellow." I wondered if Detective Club was on the case.

"But the person who killed him didn't possess the fine skills you possessed."

What an odd thing to say. "So, do you condemn what was done to him?"

"No, he was torturing you, wasn't he?"

He had me there. "Yeah, I could forgive the person who killed him."

"There's something else," Greg said in a hushed tone.

Stop beating around the bush, would ya? Just fucking tell me, I wanted to scream. "Oh, and what might that be?"

"Doctor Ellensworth was killed too!"

"This must be my lucky day! What happened to that bitch?"

"They found her hanging in her bedroom with one of her belts. There was a suicide note that said she was wrong to have an affair with Steve, a.k.a., Mr. Orderly."

"I knew those two were getting it on! What a sec, how the hell do you know all of this information? I've been online, and hadn't found anything about their deaths."

"The upper management is keeping it a secret, and they heavily monitor what sites you visit when you're online. But I have a friend, who has a friend, which works in the police department."

I started to sweat. My gnarled hands hurt just thinking about my next question I was going to pose to Greg. "Your friend wouldn't be Detective Jay Club, would it? Because if it is, we can't be friends."

"Oh no! I don't like him either. My friend's friend doesn't work at the same station, but knows who he is, and she told me he was an ass."

A thought occurred to me. "Greg, how do I know you're not an inmate like me, or that crazy woman, Chelst, and you're just impersonating an orderly? You have the white shirt, white pants with the white shoes, but that could be easily obtainable if you had family on the outside."

"You don't. And I'm not an orderly. Neither was Mr. Orderly. He was a nurse. So am I. Mr. Orderly was just his last name."

"Mr. Orderly a nurse? That's a difficult concept to comprehend. Okay, say you're correct and you're a nurse. Did you come here to introduce yourself? Did you come to torture me? What are your intentions with me?" Folks, I had a right to know these things.

"I came here to introduce myself to you, and to give you an ultimatum."

I knew it. There was always silver in a golden

lining. Here comes the Karma part I was telling you about. "What type of ultimatum?"

He walked to the door, opened up, looked left and right, and came back to me. "I want you to teach me how to remove body parts."

Laughter escaped my lips. "You want me to train you on how to procure body parts? And if I said no?"

Greg pushed me onto my bed. He leaned in close. "Then I will make your life a living hell far worse than Mr. Orderly ever did to you!"

"I seriously doubt that would be possible, Greg."

Greg smiled. His face grinned until I thought his teeth would come out of his mouth. "Did Mr. Orderly ever take his baton and shove it up your ass?"

"He threatened to, but never actually did it."

Greg took hold of me, lifted me up, turned me around, and threw me on my bed. I was lying on my chest. He went underneath me, and undid my string to my pajamas, and pulled my pants down.

"What the fuck are you doing? Stop!"

"I am proving a point. I will take this baton, and shove it up your ass. Is that what you want?"

"Hell, no!"

"Then are we clear who is in charge here?"

"You are! You are! Just get that fucking thing away from me!"

Greg taunted me by smacking my ass with the baton. "Good. I am going to let you get up, but make no mistake, if you don't do what I say, I will do far worse things to you!"

Wow, this dude was crazy, dear readers! I got up, shook the fear off me, and sat down. "Greg, why me? Any tissue procurement specialist can do what I did. Some, like a circulator I knew, was even better than me."

"Ben, it's not like I can go to the nearest tissue bank and ask someone to teach me that skill. You're here, and you're going to help me learn. I want you to scout people out, and tell me which person would be good to take grafts from."

I chuckled for several seconds. "Greg, I am confined to this nuthouse. I am not even allowed to go outside. Why? I don't know. It's not like I can jump a fence to escape, or run. The only exercise I get is when I go to rehabilitation, and let me tell you that is painful."

"Ben, I will take care of everything. I just need to know you're on board."

"Okay, okay, I am on board, it's not like I have much of a choice, now do I? But how do I disguise my face?" God, I went from someone that was feared throughout Indiana, to a wuss that took commands from a psycho nurse.

He looked at me. "That mustardness does make it difficult. How did you do it when you were in your prime?"

"My prime? I'm only twenty- seven! I wore an oversize hoodie, and sunglasses. Why?"

"Well, my most prized possession, I want you to take me out on the streets, show me who to abduct, and teach me to procure from them."

I came to the conclusion that Greg now owned me. "Dead or alive?"

"Alive, of course! Are you getting soft on me, Ben?"

"Wouldn't dream of it. Since this seems to be a mandatory thing from here on in, what's in it for me?"

Greg crossed his arms. "What do you want?"

"I want more freedom to stroll through the halls. There are certain people that despise me, and have made my life more difficult here."

"Just name them, and I will see they never bother you again."

"Okay, here are the people." I verbally named them, and he wrote them down. Didn't know, or care how he got rid of them, not my problem. My problem was Greg, and how he planned on getting the both of us off the grounds without anyone knowing about it. Well, wish me good luck as I commence on this adventure. Tissue procurement, here we go again.

July 20th

A week went by without another peep from Greg. I saw him around, taking care of patients, making sure I was tended to, but he never brought up our arrangement. It was nice while it lasted. I was free from fear for the first time in my life. I walked through the corridors without incident, or snide remarks. Alas, all good things must come to an end.

I don't recall what afternoon he came into my room. All days went by as a blur. He woke me up out of a deep sleep.

"Wakie, wakie! It's time for my first lesson!"

I grudgingly got up and noticed Greg had a bag with him. "What's in the brown paper bag? Medical supplies?"

He looked at his bag, and laughed. "No, since I am in the training stages, there won't be a need for your infamous medical bag of tricks. There's something special in here that I will show you later on."

"But, you need medical equipment so I can teach you sterile techniques or you won't be doing it correctly."

"You can explain it to me while we're harvesting."

"Greg, I'm a stickler for details. We'll need a wide array of medical instruments, back table covers, a dermatome, shall I go on?"

"The dermatome, the back table covers, and the instruments will be mailed to you."

"Mailed? To me? What are you talking about? They're not going to send that stuff to a sanitarium! And they sell that stuff online?"

"Yes, you wouldn't believe what you can buy online. They're going to send it to your mother's house. I will intercept it, and then bring it here."

"But we can't do any procuring without them."

"Relax, Ben. I have a scalpel from the infirmary. We can start by slicing people open."

"But skin comes first in any procedure, Greg! We'll need a dermatome, and soap, mineral oil, etc."

"I can get the soap, mineral oil, and whatever is on the list that you're going to make me right now."

Clearly Greg has not thought this out. "Greg, don't get mad and beat me senseless, but I can't do this without the necessary tools. With skin, you don't use a scalpel, you need a dermatome."

"If it's just a practice run, why do we need anything?"

"Because Greg, if the reason you're doing this was to make extra cash through an anonymous client, they expect certain protocols to be instituted. One of those protocols is sterility; the second is the necessary order of grafts taken. The third is packaging of said body parts, and there's more."

"Why do we need to take grafts in a certain order?"

"Because of contamination. If you want to take out the hip bone first, but accidentally nick the bowels just above it, you've contaminated everything, and nothing can be procured. If you took out a right femur, and put it on the left side of the person before taking another graft, you've just contaminated the femur and the left side. You have to think this through."

Greg remained silent for a minute. "I don't have a client. I wanted to do it for fun. But I see where you're going with this. Let me ask you something Ben, if I gave you access to your old email account, can you get in touch with your old client?"

"I don't know, even if I did, I am unsure if they would respond."

"It's lucky for you that you didn't know who they were. How was the police unable to trace those emails?"

"I don't know. The client probably saw me on the news, and had someone wipe out their location on their end? I'm not an expert. But I am wondering if someone is monitoring that particular email address?"

"Okay, let me deal with that issue. All right Ben, you convinced me that we need more preparation. I will let you know when I have the supplies."

"You still haven't told me what was in that bag if it wasn't medical supplies."

"Oh don't worry, you'll find out soon enough!"

Oh boy, dear readers, I was apprehensive!

July 30th

Several days elapsed. My heart raced and my nerves grew taut after each successive day Greg did not wake me up. My appetite decreased, and I was losing weight. Picture this scenario, if you will. I am at the mercy of a psycho nurse, who at any given time can make my life hell. I am forever stuck in this hellhole, and that nurse owned me. I have to do anything he said. I don't expect a pity party from you, dear readers, but I don't exactly have a bunch of friends, even insane ones here, that I can talk to. All I have is you people who will read this journal of my exploits, both good and bad. The good was when I was free, and on top of the world procuring parts from people, and making good money on the side. The challenge of the chase, the look in all those people's eyes, and the fear I inflicted upon them before I killed them! The bad is getting caught, having to deal with Mr. Orderly, the inmates, the other staff, and now Greg Hebert.

It's past midnight. This will be a short entry. I am stressed.

August 5th

The time finally came. Greg woke me up, very excited. "Get up, you lazy bum! The packages arrived!"

I wiped my eyes and yawned. "You went to my old house? Did you see my mother?"

"Yeah, looked in the window, she was cackling while watching some TV show. Has she ever visited you here?"

"No, and I don't expect her to. I would decline seeing her. She would probably ask for money, or want me to trade something of mine for cigarettes and alcohol."

Greg threw the packages on my bed. "Open them, Ben. Tell me if I have everything."

I gave him a sarcastic look while I put up my deformed hands. "I can barely dress myself, let alone open up packages."

Greg laughed as he took out a large pocket knife from his pants pocket.

"Carefully, Greg. If you slice a back table cover, it will no longer be sterile."

He looked at me and nodded. He carefully opened up of the boxes. I saw a dermatome inside a case, instruments for procuring skin and bones, veins, and the heart. Plus several boxes of back table covers, mineral oil, and other assortment of stuff we would need. Perfect. I was getting that warm fuzzy feeling before I used to go out and scour for my next victim.

"Do you have a victim in mind, Greg?"

He looked up from the instruments and eyeballed me. "No, I was going to give you the honors. Do you have someone in mind?"

I mulled it over in my head. Yup, he would do. "Yes, AJ Mandary."

"Who is that?"

"A couple of years ago, he was a nurse that worked in the surgery department at a large hospital in Indianapolis. I implicated him twice in the murders of two of my victims. I don't know if he was ever convicted or not. Since I was caught in the act of surgically removing lots of body parts from Jay Club's girlfriend, Brittany Schott, he was either let loose, or stopped becoming a suspect.

"But why him, after all this time?"

"Because our first victim would be a trial and

192

error mission. I know where he used to work; we can drive there, and see if he still works there."

"I don't know, Ben. It's a long shot."

"Trust me on this one, Greg. He used to leave work at seven PM. We could leave here at six fifteen, and be there in plenty of time to scope out the parking lot."

"We can't leave that late."

"Late? What are you talking about, Greg? Seven isn't late. It doesn't even get dark until nine."

"For us to leave undetected, I made certain arrangements with people to ignore our departure. We have a window from two pm until seven pm. But we have to be back just before seven."

I got up and walked around my small room. I sat down on the one the chairs at the table that had my laptop on it. "I have to be honest; I don't like that idea because I don't really think it's a good idea going on a hunt in broad daylight."

"Why, would that change our victim, Ben? And remember, don't fuck me on this."

"It might, I won't lie. How about this idea. We go to the hospital, and wait in the parking lot. I would imagine people would be leaving after three. Perhaps we can pick out a suitable candidate that we both can agree upon?"

"Why don't we go to a more populated area, like the mall that you used to go to?"

"Two reasons. One is my face. If the police happened to be there, or someone recognized me, I'm done for, and so would you. And the second one is I no longer can take crowds. At someone's house, a parking lot that not many people come out at a time, sure. But a huge mall with thousands of bodies in close quarters? No thanks!"

"Let me explain something right now, Ben. Should we get caught, and I have an opportunity to scram, I will leave you. You will not tell on me because you would have to go back to this place," Greg pointed around my room, "And I will fuck with you every day. If I somehow lose my job, I will find a way in here, Ben, and kill you. Tell me you believe me right here, right now."

I totally believed him! "Oh yeah, I believe you! I believe you!"

"Good," Greg said as he looked at his watch. "It's a little after two, let's go to the hospital."

I got up, ready to do my part and train Greg. I walked past Greg, but he put out his hand and stopped me. "Remember our deal. You will take the blame should something occur."

"Yes, I remember. Now, will you please step aside?"

Greg smiled. I hated when he did that. "Just one more thing, then we will leave."

"Sure, what is it?" I asked with apprehension.

"The bag you've asked me about a while back? The one you thought had medical supplies in it? Look inside, it's for you. Think of it as a gift."

I gingerly walked to where the large brown papered bag was on the floor. I was able to grab the handle and bring it to the bed. Opening it proved a bit difficult, but I did it. "What the fuck is this? No way, Greg! No way!"

Greg came over and smacked me on the back of my head while he laughed. "Sure, you will. Now put them on!"

I took out a long blonde wig, a string of pearls, a woman's turtleneck sweater, a pair of jeans, and a pair of girlie shoes. There was a makeup kit too. There was even a bra in there with two oranges. "The oranges are supposed to be my tits?"

Dear readers, if you could've seen Greg laugh, you would have joined in. But I was pissed. "What the hell am I, your fucking date? C'mon Greg, seriously?"

"Look Ben, you have the mustard skin discoloration. We can't afford to take any chances of getting caught. I have a pair of scrubs I will put on, so it looks like I work there. And if they think the ugly person next to me is my girlfriend, so be it." After he completed his last sentence, he burst out laughing again.

I yelled internally. I took my malformed hands, grabbed my pillow, and screamed at the top of my lungs with my mouth pressed to the pillowcase. God, I didn't want to do this! It wasn't part of the plan! "Look Greg, I am really, really against this!"

He smile faded. His brows creased as he pointed to me. "Put the stuff on... now."

"How about a compromise?"

"What sort of compromise?"

"I get to stay in the car while identifying the targets. Once we make our selection, follow him or her, then when it's recovery time, I will get out of the car wearing this crap."

He seemed to mull over my request. "Okay."

"What about the makeup. My hands won't be able to put anything on."

"I'm not putting makeup on you, dude."

"Can we skip the makeup?"

"NO!"

"Why?"

"Because if someone sees you from afar, they would be able to give police a description of you and your mustardness."

"Shit, shit, shit!"

"I'm leaving now to put on my scrubs, and make sure our departure is still good with the people I paid off. Start undressing, and put on the other clothing, and makeup. Do your best with the makeup." He left the room laughing.

Dear readers, I was stuck. It took me some time to take my clothes off. To say I have never, ever put a bra on would be an understatement. I had never even taken one off a woman. I studied the bra, found the metal clips, and realized they got put into the hooks. Huh, so that's how women did it. I think Greg got the smallest freaking bra he could find. I bet the thing was a training bra, it was so small! It was tight on me, and I am not that big. It was a pain in the ass to insert the stupid oranges inside the cups of the bra. The oranges kept falling to the carpet. And to bend down with those extremely tight girl pants to get them, I tell ya, I was yelling! Pulling up a pair of girl jeans that didn't conform to my body type was excruciatingly painful. My hands were throbbing after forcing the pants up to my man hips. I managed to put my undershirt back on, and put on, with difficulty, the blue turtleneck sweater. I barely managed putting on the pearls. I opted to put the wig on first before applying makeup. Listen to my reasoning for this, folks. Putting the stupid wig on first would obscure part of my face, thus allowing me to put less makeup on.

I had a hard time opening the makeup kit with my hands. At least Greg bought me a large brush to put on something called a foundation. Since I had a blonde wig, I decided to put a lighter shade of foundation on. I used what was called an application sponge to put the light brown foundation on my face. I only did areas that the wig did not hide on my face. The turtleneck helped hide my throat so I wouldn't have to put makeup on there. I refused to put on eyeliner, or blush, and whatever else was in the bag. That was all I was willing to do.

Several minutes after I completed the metamorphosis, Greg entered my room, took one look at me, and laughed. "You are one ugly girl, you know that, Ben?"

"Tell me about it."

"You forgot to put on lipstick."

"Really? Lipstick? Don't you think this charade has gone far enough?"

Greg went to the bed, rummaged through the items, and found a light red lipstick. "Put it on, and I will ignore the fact that you didn't put blush or eyeliner on."

Wow, this guy was sharp. He didn't miss a thing. Reluctantly I applied the red substance to my lips. Greg looked me over, and nodded. "Let's go."

The hallways looked as though they were cleared. No one was stirring, and all the doors were closed. How Greg had managed to clear our path was dubious to me, but I was more than eager to walk through the front door. I hadn't been outside in over two years. Before we go to the door Greg handed me an old woman's coat. It was an ugly brown, and furry. I looked at him. "It's July, it's in the middle of the afternoon, and it's hot outside."

"Okay, I was just trying to bring you into character."

"Whose nasty coat was that?"

"My mother's."

"Oh, sorry," I said meekly.

"No, you're not."

When we went outside, the heat took my breath away. So, this is what fresh air felt like? It had been so long. I took a few deep inhales, and got into Greg's car. We sped away toward the unknown. I was nervous, and I could tell Greg was too. The last sentence he spoke to me before we drove out of the parking lot of the sanitarium was, "You need to walk more like a girl."

August 10th

I hadn't time lately to write in this journal, dear readers. I have been doing more therapy on my hands, and they are improving slowly. The setback from Mr. Orderly's baton attack on my hands was starting to mend. Other than that, I am still here at the sanatorium. I reread the entire contents of my journal. I realized, after the fact, I should have listened to myself, and just taken the beating from Greg, and not go out and try to resurrect my former career. And here's why.

By the time we got to the hospital, it was after three. I hadn't realized the town of McCordsville had grown so much. The traffic was horrendous. By the time we got to the hospital there were empty spaces near the front of the lot, but I told him to go further down to where I had seen AJ the last time I was here. We found a few empty spots. I suggested a spot the furthest away, and to my amazement, Greg agreed.

We waited and waited. At quarter after three several guys walked out the door. I no longer had my binoculars, and hadn't thought to ask Greg to get one. Some of the guys got into their cars, and left. As they passed us, I looked in their cars. No AJ. Three guys were about twenty yards from us. I could hear their conversation.

"What are you doing tonight, Ray?"

"I don't know, George. It depends on the wife. You know how that goes."

The guy behind them was trying to hurry up to catch up with them. "Hey Kramer, hold up!"

The thinner guy slowed down to let his friend catch up. "Sorry, Shotwell, I mean Corey. Why are you using my last name? Do I ever call you Shotwell? Or do I ever call Ray by his last name of Wininger?"

I turned to Greg. "So we have a Ray Wininger, a George Kramer, and a Corey Shotwell."

"But no AJ. How about one of those three guys? Which one do you want to abduct? The guy named Ray, Corey, or this George Kramer guy?"

I looked at the three guys. No other people were entering or exiting the building. "All three are viable candidates, but it would be foolish to try to take all three of them, even two of them at the same time."

Greg nodded.

"The guy named George Kramer is the thinnest. Maybe even the weakest of the three. What about him?" I asked earnestly.

Greg started to drum his fingers on the steering wheel. "While I agree with you, I want to have some fun. George doesn't look like he would put up as much of a struggle as Corey or Ray."

"True, but he would be the easiest target. So then, which is it, George, Corey or Ray?" I asked.

"Well Corey has a thick gray beard, so he's probably older than George or Ray. He wouldn't put up much of a struggle as I want. I want the person to fear me," Greg said with seriousness.

Greg had control issues. I would've taken the George dude, but it was his call. "Okay, that leaves the guy named Ray."

"Now that we've determined who were going to fuck up tonight, what's next?" Greg asked.

"We will follow him at a discreet distance, and see where he lives. If his wife is home, and they have kids, we have to abort the mission for today."

"But I wanted to do something today. You know how much money this is costing me right now?"

"I'm sure it's a lot, Greg. But we need to be patient so we don't get caught. I am trying to instill patience in you. Before I was asking you questions about Corey, George, and Ray so you can familiarize yourself with the type of questions and observations that you need to ask yourself."

"So it's not I see this person, let me abduct him or her, remove their parts type of thing."

I chuckled. "Far from it. You have to be meticulous and methodical."

Corey walked by our car and ignored us. Good. George's car was a lot closer. I saw his vehicle as he opened his door. There was a car magnet that said something about an Arcadis fantasy series of books he had written. Maybe I should look up George Kramer online, and see if he could give me any advice on how to publish my journal. Maybe even buy his books.

Ray's car was even closer than George's. He paid us no attention as he got in, started his car, and pulled away. I waited until both Ray and George left the parking lot, then told Greg to follow Ray's car.

Ray was a slow driver. He's one of the few people that actually did the speed limit. We stayed a few car lengths back as not to draw any attention. I checked the sky. The sun was shining, and there wasn't a cloud in the sky. "Greg, I've never done recoveries during the day unless I am working at the tissue bank. Doing during the day scares me."

"Don't be such a pussy," he said with vehemence in his voice.

I decided I had to rattle his cage. "Greg, I'm serious. People will see two strangers either parked in his driveway, or walking to his house in broad daylight, and then we'll have all of our medical equipment. Don't you think people will notice that, and become suspicious?"

He grew silent. I hope my words sunk it because as we were pulling in Ray's neighborhood, my angst increased. After a few tense minutes, Greg finally spoke. "You may be right. Maybe I didn't think this afternoon thing all the way through. But we're here. Maybe all we need to do is bring a scalpel, and you can show me where to start the initial incision?"

My dubiousness was apparent. I looked around. Kids were everywhere, on the lawns, in the streets, on their stoops. "I have a bad feeling about this, Greg."

He sat more erect. He wiped his brow. "Okay, how about just for today, we just have some fun. You be my bitch, we just walk up to Ray's house, and make up a story. It works in the movies all the time!"

"I know it works, because I've used a cover story before. Still," I said as I again peered down the long road that Teed off, "I am apprehensive."

"You better say yes fast because people are going to start to notice us."

I scanned the interior of his car. "Do you have anything in here that we could fool Ray with to sell to him?"

"I don't know, all the medical shit's in here. Let's try the trunk."

Odd he wouldn't know what was in his car. I knew every square inch inside and out of mine, when I could drive, and owned a vehicle. But I was a professional worrywart. Greg didn't seem to care one way or another. "Why don't you go to the trunk, and I'll wait in here."

We were parked two doors down from Ray's house. Greg got out of the car, turned off the engine, and said, "Why?"

"Because of you, I am dressed like a fucking female. Men do stuff for women. Well, most of them do. Plus, we made the arrangement that I wouldn't be seen until we were ready. Clearly we are not."

"All right." He pointed at me. "Don't go anywhere, or do anything to draw attention to yourself, got me?"

I crossed my heart. Where the hell was I going to

go? I could probably drive this contraption, but inadvertently getting pulled over would not bode well for me.

I could hear Greg rummaging through the trunk, pushing things aside, throwing stuff. Good way not to get noticed, Greg. I wouldn't dare say that to him, but I thought it.

"Aha! Found something!" Greg yelled to me.

"Why don't you just scream it so everyone can hear you?"

"What did you say to me?" He demanded as he opened up my side of the car.

I had to remain calm. I think Greg had the capacity to kill me right here and now, and not suffer any remorse. "You are acting like a newbie! We need to be discreet! Please don't yell, or do anything that will attract attention to us. You've been loud since we parked here. For the love of god, would you just listen to me?" I beat my one of semi-useless hands on my thin chest. "I have done this before, I know what to look for, and how to act, and you're doing the exact opposite!"

"I know, I know. You're right."

"Look at these malformed hands. These are the

result of not being totally prepared, and getting caught."

"Okay, I get it! Can we just move on?"

Wow, that was almost an apology. "Sure. What did you find in the trunk?"

Greg smiled. Dear readers, I've told you I hated when he smiled, right? He walked back to the end of the car, and came back with an old, beaten down basketball. "What are we going to do with that? Are you going to challenge the kids? Darn, I don't think I can run in these girly shoes."

I sensed it before it struck. I figured I used up his last nerve was my thought as the punch hit me squarely in the jaw. My head snapped, and the wig shifted position on my head. I knew that because I could no longer see. "Enough of the sarcasm, okay? We're going to go to Ray's house, knock on the door, and ask him if he lost the basketball."

I tried to feel my jaw. It was numb. I looked in the mirror and straightened my ridiculous wig. The damn thing didn't even look real! "Um… okay."

"I sense you don't approve."

"We don't know if he has any kids."

"Exactly, Ben. That way we can find out if he's home alone or not. We could say our son brought it home. We told him it belonged to the rightful owner, and our son said he found it on Ray's lawn. Perfect!"

So now I am not only dressed like a girl, but Greg and I have a child. A son to be exact. "What's our son's name, in case Ray asks so we can be on the same page?" This set up couldn't get any wackier, that is, until I heard the name.

"How about Zaner?"

"Nah, I always liked the names Spencer or Ian."

"Our child's name is Zaner. Now let's go. We've been here way too long."

"Fine!" I hissed as I got out of the air conditioned car, and into the stifling heat. "My makeup better not run before we get to the house," I whispered in fury.

After several steps I asked Greg, "do you have the scalpel, or did you take anything else?"

Greg hastened his steps and I followed suit. He patted his back pocket with one hand, and held the basketball with the other. "Just the scalpel."

"Even if the cap is still on, make sure you don't sit on that blade, or you'll have a laceration the size of

New Jersey on your ass."

We got to Ray's house. It was a large, two story house with gray siding. I noticed a chimney. I pointed to it, and said, "Looks like Ray has a fireplace. Maybe we should burn down his house after we done with him."

"Now that's the Ben I've heard so much about. We can certainly do that if you want."

"It would be fun, but like I stated earlier, it's just too light outside."

"Always the party pooper," Greg said as he knocked on the door.

He knocked gingerly a few more times until we heard the door unlock, and open. "Can I help you?" At least he was friendly and polite.

Greg started out friendly, something I was happy about. "Yes, sir. Our son, Zaner (I caught him glancing at me), found this basketball, and told us it came from this yard. We wanted to return it to its rightful owner."

Ray looked the ball over, as I took a good look at him. He was taller than me and Greg, but not by much. His brown hair was shoulder length and he had broad shoulders. For me to take him on when I did tissue, I would have had to have the element of surprise. Greg didn't seem fazed. He also had the use of both his hands, unlike me.

"No, I can't say it's mine. My wife and daughter are gone, so I can't ask them."

I felt my makeup drip. If we didn't get inside soon, Ray would find out the truth. "Sir, can I use your bathroom?" I said in the most girly voice I could muster. God, I am going to be the laughing stock of the sanatorium. I'm sure Greg will somehow exploit the situation.

"Sure, help yourself. Anything for a pretty lady." He opened the door wider to let us both through. Ray must need glasses if he thought I was pretty in this idiotic outfit, and the smeared makeup. He pointed to the right, and I made a beeline to it, while trying in vain to walk like a girl. Jesus, they should give people lessons on how to walk in these things. And these weren't even high heels!

I did my best to clean myself up, and use the restroom. And dear readers, I always wore gloves, if you recall. I had them in my really tight back pocket. I took several pairs. I like to err on the side of caution. I put a pair on then I took a piss, flushed, and walked back to where the front door was. Only Greg and Ray weren't there. I heard some muffled noises, and headed in that direction. I walked through Ray's spacious kitchen, took a step down, and walked to the living room. There was Ray, shirtless, and pant-less, tied up. Greg, for his part, was all smiles.

"Well, that was quick," I remarked in earnest.

"Wait, you talked like a dude. You're a dude? Man, why are you dressed up like a girl?" Ray asked with disgust in his voice.

"Don't ask, I won't tell. How did you get to tie him up, Greg?"

"Don't use my real name! Damn we should have come up with some cool code names."

"Greg, the purpose of this exercise was to find people, and learn how to remove body parts. Ray isn't going to be telling anyone anything. So, how did you get him tied up so fast?"

"I knocked him on the side of the head with a metal meat tenderizer I found while we were talking in the kitchen. I grabbed it while he wasn't looking, and when we entered the living room, I smashed it over his head. He's bleeding a little in the back of his head."

To think I used to be the one to do the smashing. "Great work! This is bringing back memories." I turned to Ray. "You're going to die tonight, but I have a few questions for you first."

"I'm not afraid of dying, girl man."

"Cute. Ray, do you know AJ Mandery?"

"Why?"

"Just answer the question."

"I want to know why too," Greg stated. He was leaning on a chair watching our exchange.

I looked at Greg. "Should you graduate from my teachings, grasshopper, you'll find I either ask, or talk to all of my victims. You know kind of get to know them first, kill them later."

"What's the point of that? Let's just slice him open, and be done with it," Greg told me menacingly.

"It's the psychological aspect to the game I play, Greg. It's disarming, they think I won't do anything to them, and then I lay it out to them what's going to happen."

"Then what?"

"Then they usually start to cry, or beg for mercy."

"Hmm, I'll have to make a mental note about that one."

For his part, Ray was the perfect host. But he didn't seem too scared. "Why aren't you frightened of us, Ray?"

"I've made peace with my maker a long time ago."

I walked up to him, and tried the best I could to slap him. There wasn't any force behind my slap, not with my hands. "So noble of you, Ray!"

I saw Greg roll his eyes. He stopped leaning over the chair, walked in front of Ray, and repeatedly punched him in the face. Ray took it like a man, and spit out blood.

"Ben, how are we going to stop him from screaming?"

"What did you do with his socks?"

"Those nasty things? I threw them out."

"Go get them from the garbage, then stuff them in his mouth!"

Greg went to get them without complaint. When he came back he had a look of disgust.

"What is it?" I asked.

"There were some nasty looking burritos in the

garbage. A lot of it went on his smelly socks."

"Perfect, shove those bad boys in his mouth!"

Ray tried to resist, but eventually the burritos socks went in his mouth. I went to the kitchen, and opened up a few drawers. Most people have a junk drawer where they keep miscellaneous items in there. I was looking for tape. I found the drawer on my fourth attempt. I took out a large piece of tape, and tapped his mouth shut.

To his credit, Greg took out the scalpel and was teasing Ray. He pretended to thrust the blade on Ray's face, chest, and abdomen.

To my trained eye, I saw two mistakes. There were a lot more since we didn't have all the necessary tools and supplies, but these two mere mandatory. "Greg, two important things I noticed that have to be rectified. One is more important than the other."

"Okay, shoot."

"The first thing I just noticed is you're not wearing any gloves. You've been all over this house. That means your fingerprints are all over the place!"

"And the second thing?" He asked as if he didn't care what I just said.

"I'm still trying to understand your reaction to my first question. Oh well, it's your life. The second question is more like a statement. I think you should lay Ray down on the floor. Still keep him tied up, but he needs to be on the ground for a better recovery."

"Okay." Greg took hold of Ray, and shoved him to the side. Ray fell on his left side. I went over there, and took my foot, and pushed his side until Ray was on his back, facing us.

Ray looked up at me, and didn't try to utter a word, or try to wiggle himself free. It was like he knew whatever he did or said, wasn't going to change the situation. It wouldn't have, but it would've been nice to see.

"Okay Greg, go to either side of Ray, and bend down."

"Don't you usually do them on a table?"

"At work, yes. Somewhere else, whatever is available."

Greg knelt beside Ray. He had the scalpel in his right hand. "Okay, I'm ready. Where do I start?"

"Go about four inches above the hipbone. Start making the incision slowly and go slow as you go down toward his kneecap."

Greg started slow enough, but he did a couple of things wrong. "Hey Greg! Hold up! First, you started off slow, but you're going too fast! And second, you're going way too deep! If you were taking out the saphenous veins, you would have destroyed them, or the fascia!" Blood was pooling on the floor from his thigh to past his kneecap.

"Oh sorry, I didn't realize what I was doing. I was looking at the pained expression on Ray's face!"

Got to admit it, Greg was correct. Ray's face was contorted in pain. His eyes were squeezed shut, and his body tried to compensate by convulsing. "You have to stop the convulsing!"

"How?" He started to panic.

"Don't have an anxiety attack, Greg! It's all right. Just tie him to something so tight that he can't move."

Greg tried in vain too, but the seizure continued. "Quick, go in his garage, and look for something, anything that might stop him!" I yelled. I didn't care if Ray convulsed or not, but it was fun watching Greg have a panic attack. A few minutes later, Greg came back with a saw. Not just a saw, but a small hacksaw. "What the hell are you going to do with that thing?"

"What does it look like? I am going to hack off

his leg!"

"No, I have a better idea!"

Greg's eyes bulged out. "What? Why can't I cut off the leg? It will stop the nerves from sending signals down there!"

"Greg, why don't you stop sending signals totally from Ray?"

That did not perk up Ray. He shook his head back and forth. He didn't know what I meant. "What do you mean?"

"Take the hacksaw, saw his frontal bone, or his forehead back and forth until you go all the way through his brain, and out the other side. That will stop all the signals!'"

"Great idea, Ben. I knew your old self would come back!"

Ray didn't seem to like the idea. Too fucking bad.

Dear readers, despite me not giving a shit that Ray's head was gradually being hack-sawed off, never in a million years would I do that to someone because I have my standards. But Greg? Hell no. I watched in fascination as he took the hacksaw and placed it between Ray's eyes and his hairline. With

Ray trying to turn his head away from the saw, it had the opposite effect. The hacksaw started digging into his forehead. He realized what he was doing, so he stopped moving his head back and forth. Ray tried to look up but the blood slowly dripped in his eyes. Greg emitted a chuckle, pressed firmly, and started going back and forth. The further Greg pressed in, the more blood poured forth. Back and forth he went. As the front cranial was being exposed, it made sounds akin to wood being cut. But the smell was altogether different. It smelled of burning flesh, and it smelled wonderful! It brought me back to the days of taking out people's knee blocks or whole legs with the Gigli saw. The redolence was reminiscent of days that I will never capture again, because now I was the one that was captured.

Rays muffled screaming lessened, then stopped as his brain was now the target of the saw. The gray matter was much more pliable and flexible, almost spongy. As Greg worked through the brain, pieces of it flew in all directions. Blood soaked his clothes because we didn't bring any P.P.E. Sloppy Greggie, sloppy. But I wasn't going to tell him that he's left enough evidence for a police officer's wet dream. I told him about putting on gloves, and he put them on after he'd been all over the house.

I was watching Greg but my attention started to wane. I had enough. The fun was over. I was about to tell him he'd done enough damage when the front door opened. Ray's wife looked at us, looked at Ray, and dropped the grocery bags she was carrying. She ran outside as she was frantically searching her pocketbook. I knew she was looking for the phone to call the police.

"I thought Ray told us she wasn't coming here until later!" Greg yelled.

I looked at him disbelievingly. "Evidently he lied. Maybe he sensed something was wrong when he let us in with that stupid basketball fiasco."

"Go after her, Ben!"

"At this point, she's already made the call, I can guarantee it."

"Remember what I said to you! You take the blame! All of it! I have to find some of Ray's clothes before I leave. I can't go with all of this blood on me."

"Yeah, you're right about that," I said with disinterest.

"Oh, and by the way, go through the house, and get rid of any of my fingerprints!"

"Are you serious? I don't know where you've been, Greg!"

"Then I guess you'll just have to do the whole house, now won't you?"

I looked at him as if he had lost his mind, because I really think at that point, he had. To placate him, because I had no intention of doing any of that nonsense, I said, "Sure Greg! Now hurry up! I'm sure the police are on their way!" I knew I was done for. And when, not if, Greg got caught, I would tell him I was in the process of removing any and all traces of his fingerprints, they're just wasn't enough time.

Dear readers, I could hear the sirens coming closer and closer. This would make it the second time I got caught. Hopefully no one will put any of my parts in a vice grip this time around.

September 2nd

This will be my last entry for some time as I acclimatize to sanatorium life again, and I am almost up to date on what happened after Greg escaped. Much time had elapsed.

Folks, the police came in droves. I put up my hands in surrender as soon as they got into the house. I had time to remove the wig, the makeup, and the clothing, but it would've made the headlines regardless. So I said fuck it. They put handcuffs on me, and tightened them until I couldn't feel anything. As they were escorting me out of the house, I had a chance to see a rookie cop throw up his lunch.

At the police station, I was interrogated, and told on Greg Hebert. Why, after I was threatened repeatedly not to tell on him? Because of all the damned evidence he had left behind. I warned him not to do anything when the sun was out, but he wouldn't listen. They put out an APB on him. It was only a matter of time until they caught him.

And what happened to me? If you noticed, much time had elapsed with the dates of the journal.

The interrogation led them nowhere because I admitted everything. I told them I was a patient at the sanatorium in McCordsville, and if they wanted to speak with the Warden, Mr. Jack Phillips, he would confirm my identity. They told me they knew quite well who I was (after I took off the wig and the makeup). I overheard some of the officers saying Detective Jay Club was made cognizant of the situation. He wanted to come to the station but thankfully they drove me back to the sanatorium after confirming with Mr. Phillips that I did reside there. The handcuffs were removed as I entered the facility. Mr. Phillips told them he would take care of me from here on in.

Mr. Phillips brought me to his office. His large desk encompassed three quarters of the room. There were pictures of him shaking hands and smiling with a few celebrities, and of other official looking people. He walked over to his chair, sat, and motioned me to sit at the small chair. "Ben, were you coerced in helping Greg with those gruesome acts?"

"No because as I told the police there wasn't anything wrong with what we did, and I still believe that, even to this day."

Mr. Phillips became solemn. "Why did you get involved with Greg?"

I looked at him disbelievingly. "It's not like I had a choice in the matter, Sir!"

His blue eyes bored into mine. "Sure, there was. You could've told Greg no."

I laughed. "You don't get it sir. I really didn't have a choice."

He straightened his posture. "Explain because I don't understand."

"Mr. Orderly used to torment me on an almost daily basis. One afternoon, some time ago, Greg Hebert walked into my room explaining Mr. Orderly was, in fact, a nurse and not an orderly like I presumed, and that he was killed at his house. The same with Mrs. Ellensworth." He said both murders were linked, and that they were lovers."

"Greg told you that?"

"Yes, yes he did."

Jack Phillips rubbed his eyes with his hands. He blew out a heavy breath. "That story is a fabrication. Mr. Orderly did not die, nor did Mrs. Ellensworth. Mr. Orderly was caught having sex with one of the patients here, so he got fired. Mrs. Ellensworth found another position closer to home. The fact both of them left almost at the same time was just a coincidence."

"Huh? Why would Greg lie to me?" I said perplexed.

"What do you know about Greg?"

"Only that he is worse than Mr. Orderly, and that he is a nurse. That's all."

Jack looked at me for some time. It seemed like he was trying to get something off his chest. "Greg Hebert is my nephew. He is not a nurse. He is a patient. He is… delusional."

"How was he able to roam freely here, and drive to Ray's house? And he told me he bribed the guards to leave the hallways free for us to leave."

"Greg may be neurotic, but he is not dumb. As a matter of fact, he's very smart. Greg is my nephew; he has more liberties than the normal inmates because of me. I wasn't aware of his bullying you, Ben. And as for the car, he stole mine. I was in a meeting. He could have taken my keys at any point in the day, and I wouldn't have known about it."

"And the guards?"

"They make minimum wage. They accept bribes, it's human nature. I will fire them too."

"Greg left a lot of evidence at the crime scene. I tried to tell him but he wouldn't listen to me. When he is found, and I assume it will be soon, will he come back here?"

225

"Of course."

"Damn!"

"Why does that concern you? I can restrict his access to your floor, if you think that would help."

"Mr. Phillips, Greg threatened me repeatedly that if he got caught, he would come after me here. He'll get by the guards, he'll come to my floor, and he will continue to torture me."

"Aren't you being a little melodramatic, Ben?"

I showed him the burn mark on my armpit, and several other areas where I had been knocked around. "Your nephew will be worse than Mr. Orderly."

His face softened. "I'm sorry about Mr. Orderly but I can assure you, no, guarantee, that Greg will never go near you here ever again."

"How can you guarantee such a preposterous statement? It's inconceivable to me that you would have that level of control over someone like him."

"Ben, I don't like your attitude. Suffice to say, you're just going to have to trust me."

I left after that ludicrous statement. At least for the time being I could travel the halls without fear of

Greg appearing out of nowhere. I climbed the stairs, and noticed feces were spread on the handrail. My hand was encased in fresh poop. "Ewww!" I yelled. Someone nearby snickered. I heard footsteps run away. I went up one more flight of stairs, found the restroom, and washed my hands over and over again. I used hot water, as hot as I could get it to feel that the fecal matter was off my hand. I looked up, and the mirror had fogged. I still continued to wash it. Amazing, wasn't it dear readers? That I could take parts of the human body out, with all the blood and guts, and I was fine. But put a little poop on me, and I wigged out.

The door opened but I didn't pay attention to who entered. I causally looked up in the mirror but it was still fogged up. "Cute, putting shit on the handrail, dude!"

"Hi, Ben. We have some talking, and I have some ass kicking to do."

I turned around hesitantly. I started to shake uncontrollably. "Hi, Greg."

He took me by the scruff of my neck, squeezed hard, and forced me out of the bathroom door. "You told on me, Ben. Remember what I told you I would do to you?"

"Greg, you left evidence all over the house!"

"I told you to clean it!"

"I tried! But I didn't know everywhere you went! Plus, I told you not to do a recovery in broad daylight!"

We got to my room. He opened the door, and shoved me to the table. I hit it so hard my laptop fell. "So now everything is my fault!" He started to remove his belt.

"What are you doing, Greg?"

"I am going to give you the beating of your life with my belt."

"Can we talk about this?"

"You can talk all you want, Ben. You betrayed me."

I could see trying to cater to his irrational behavior wouldn't do any good. The first hit of his belt nailed me in my side, stung. Greg took the belt and halved it, came in closer, and hit me so hard; I could feel my back bruise instantly. I yelled from the pain.

"Stop yelling, Ben! Do you know what it's like trying to avoid the law all this time?"

"Um, yes! Do you remember who I was?"

He seemed to concede the point. "Anyway, I waited and waited until they brought you back here. Sneaking in here wasn't an easy task. I was going to hide in your room but I saw you with the Warden, Mr. Phillips. I waited and followed you to the bathroom."

"The Warden, Mr. Phillips? You mean your uncle?"

He flicked the belt so fast I had no time to react. The metal buckle smacked into my jaw. I felt the pain as my jaw started to swell immediately. It was in the same spot he had punched me in the face a few months ago in his uncle's car at Ray's house.

I put my hand to my jaw. "Greg, cut the shit!"

"Oh, and what are you going to do about it? It's not like you can hit me with your fucked up hands!"

I tried to run to the door but he nailed me in the back. Momentarily stung, I fell to my knees. He came at me and smashed his belt over and over again on my thin back. I could feel welts forming. I felt liquid dripping on my back, and realized it was my blood. After a few more hard swings he stopped, and panted for breath. He walked to my bed, and sat down. I got up with agonizing difficulty.

"Don't go anywhere, Ben. I'm not through with you. If you managed to escape, I will come in here when you're asleep, when you're beating off, or whenever the mood strikes me."

I accepted my fate when I got caught the first time. I am living with the consequences. I will accept my fate being caught the second time despite it not being my fault. But I would not, could not, let Greg continue to torture me. I have had a lifetime of misfortune, of repeated beatings, of torture, and it had to stop now. It was difficult to walk to the table. My back and side were in excruciating pain. Greg seemed pleased with himself that I did not egress the room. I bent down to the floor, retrieved the laptop, opened it, turned around, and faced Greg.

"I can show you, in my secret journal, that I had nothing to do with you being a fugitive." I turned around, hoping Greg would come to the table. I heard him get off my bed, and could feel his presence next to me.

"You would do that for me?"

"To stop the beating and to prove to you I had nothing to do with the police coming after you, yes." Now, dear readers, astute and shrewd as you are, you know I spoke in my journal that I babbled to the police about Greg's involvement. Don't you fret.

"Greg, I usually speak into the computer. Would you go to the *find and replace* button on top, and type in your name so we can go directly to that page, so I can prove to you once and for all I had nothing to do with the manhunt for you?"

Greg leaned in, looked for the button, found it, and started typing. While Greg was distracted, I took the opportunity to slam, as hard as I could muster; the top of the laptop closed on to his fingers, and used my body weight to keep the laptop closed as long as I could. He finally broke free, looked at his hands, and gave me a death stare. Quickly, I took the laptop and smashed him in the face. He twirled around. When he came at me, I hit him in the face again. He momentarily became confused. Anger and adrenaline overtook me. I took all of my strength and hit him on the top of his head. He fell to his knees. I continued to smash his nose, his eyes, his head, his throat, everywhere using every ounce of my being to render him unconscious. But I didn't stop there. I took a few minutes break, until I saw him regaining his consciousness. Nope, that wouldn't bode well for me. I took the laptop, and smashed his face again and again. When he was out cold, I knelt down, took the laptop and smashed his hand and fingers until they were unrecognizable. I did the same thing to the other side. He would never be able to hurt me or anyone ever again. I got up, sat on my bed, and waited for all hell to break loose. Inwardly I smiled.

September 4th

Last entry was supposed to be my last one but I had to tell you about Greg. He will never be able to write again, or have much use of his hands, like me. He has become the model inmate, and has become docile. I like to pretend to hit him when no one is looking and he cowers. I was able to salvage my journal after the beating it took hitting Greg.

A real nurse, by the name of Donna Perry Graybosch, started working here a couple of months ago. She's friendly, and nice. But I must tell you, dear readers, that Donna and I share a very big secret. She wants me to teach her how to procure tissue.

Made in the USA
Lexington, KY
03 March 2017